QUEEN BEA

Other Books by Margaret M. Blanchard

The Rest of the Deer: An Intuitive Study of Intuition
From the Listening Place: Languages of Intuition
Restoring the Orchard (with S.B. Sowbel): *A Guide to Learning Intuition*

Hatching (fiction)
Wandering Potatoes (fiction)
Who? (fiction)

Duet (poetry, with paintings by S.B. Sowbel)
Beyond the Keys (poetry)

Queen Bea

A Novel by Margaret M. Blanchard

iUniverse, Inc.
New York Lincoln Shanghai

Queen Bea

iUniverse books may be ordered through booksellers or by contacting:

iUniverse
2021 Pine Lake Road, Suite 100
Lincoln, NE 68512
www.iuniverse.com
1-800-Authors (1-800-288-4677)

Author photo by Kathleen Herrington
Cover photo by Margaret Blanchard

ISBN-13: 978-0-595-36338-4 (pbk)
ISBN-13: 978-0-595-80775-8 (ebk)
ISBN-10: 0-595-36338-5 (pbk)
ISBN-10: 0-595-80775-5 (ebk)

Printed in the United States of America

Thanks to the powerful women who supported the shaping of this narrative:

*Sowbel, Elizabeth Minnich, Virginia Holmes,
Jan Wilkotz, Pamela DiPesa, Roni Natov,
Judith Arcana, Bernice Mennis, Ann Blanchard*

"What does it mean that success is as dangerous as failure?
Whether you go up the ladder or down it,
Your position is shaky.
When you stand with your own two feet on the ground,
You will always keep your balance."

—*Tao Te Ching*, translated by Stephen Mitchell

"She died   a famous woman   denying
her wounds
denying
her wounds   came   from the same source as her power."

—Adrienne Rich, "Power," *The Dream of a Common Language*

"Like a bee trapped for life in the closing of the sweet flower…
She says, the single Lotus will swallow you whole."

—Mirabai, translated by Jane Hirshfield

PROLOGUE

▼

Narrative truth, according to theorist Jean-Francois Lyotard, finds its most authoritative expression in Grand Narratives, distinguished from Little Stories by their abstract heroes, their collective acceptance, and their role as myth rather than mere entertainment.

Until the current rise of scholarship about, for, and by women, Little Stories, which rise from daily and domestic life, were relegated to the female, while Grand Narratives were dominated by the male, just as traditional protagonists for Grand Narratives were of noble blood or royal status rather than mere commoners. In recent years women scholars have discovered women heroes worthy of the status of Grand Narratives, queens like Inanna, heroes like the Woman Warrior, historical figures like Harriet Tubman.

In concert with these renewed creations, I hope to explore in this novel the genre of tragedy in relation to women: the tragic hero, the tragic flaw, the tragic redemption. As women gain power, however limited it still is within abiding patriarchal systems, we face the potential of such experiences. We don't have to have royal blood or queenly status to face such reversals; we don't have to be famous or rich to discover our flaws and their often tragic consequences.

This tale combines, as many women's narratives do, the Grand and the Little, the public and the private, the boardroom and the kitchen. But it is not about my own family, nor about any particular family I know. I have written about my own family elsewhere and I abstract from the many stories I've heard about other families. This story is not even about families as such but about family as a system. Systems dynamics can apply to nations or individuals as well as to families. Struggles for power, control, respect and recognition occur within each of us individually as parallel dynamics take place within institutions. Family provides the most accessible and familiar context for such dynamics, whether they are played out in Greek amphitheaters, in the Globe Playhouse of Shakespeare's time or in contemporary movie theaters. Most patriarchal tragedies bring disaster to the whole family, whether the children are themselves infected by the greed or egoism of the father or whether they are innocent victims of his wrongful decisions. Look what happens to nations ruled by tyrants.

Many of the grandest narratives of our culture involve family dynamics, particularly relations between parents and children, the tension between generations, between what has been and what is to come. Christianity, for instance, is build upon the story of the obedient son, Jesus, who carried away on his cross the sins of his earthly family and redeemed their souls by obeying the will of his heavenly father. Buddhism, on the other hand, has as its foundation the disobedient son, who chose to leave his father's palace against his father's will, to renounce his inherited power for the mastery of meditation.

Disobedient daughters fare not so well, at least in western mythology—Eve being the prime example. But even the obedient daughter has limited success. Mary, whose Magnificat is the essence of humble acceptance, remains, even on her pedestal, even with her assumption into heaven, a handmaiden of the Lord, not a divine consort, not an independent power in herself. Her mother, Ann, holds the hidden power in more matriarchal cultures.

But there are Grand Narratives where the disobedient daughter, while suffering greatly in the process, fares better in the long run than she does in western culture. Compare three disobedient daughters, these "bad girls," as some of us contemporary feminists proudly call ourselves: Cordelia from *King Lear*, The Wayward Princess from Sufi tales, and Kuan Yin, from Buddhist mythology.

Cordelia disobeys her father by remaining silent when he demands flattery in return for a portion of his kingdom, accepting exile rather than practice greed and hypocrisy. She dies at the hands of her treacherous sisters, the innocent victim of her father's egotism, reconciled at the end with her remorseful father but lacking agency to free him or herself. She is punished for her waywardness. Both father and daughter must die.

The Wayward Princess, as told by Idries Shah, like Cordelia, has two sisters who agree when their father the king tells them that his will alone determines their future and their fate. When she, however, disagrees, he imprisons her and cuts her off from her inheritance. Upon her continued defiance, rather than execute her, he exiles her to the wilderness. Here, however, rather than languishing, the princess thrives, discovering a life in nature, among wild beasts and with other exiles, that not only does *not* depend upon the will of her father but has its own independent harmony and fruitfulness. Soon this realm of outcasts becomes renowned for its wisdom, justice, and beauty, far surpassing her father's kingdom. When the king finally visits this mysterious place, his daughter observes, "You see, Father, every man and every woman has his own fate and his own choice." This story, Shah tells us, is used in the Sufi tradition, "to illustrate the possibility of 'a different state of consciousness' in man." (*Tales of the Dervishes*, p. 65.)

This different state of consciousness in "man" is embodied in the person of Kuan Yin whose humble beginnings are described by Patricia Monaghan (*Wild Girls, p. 17*). Born Miao Shin, she chose at a young age to become a hermit rather than marry the rich man arranged by her father. Like the father in the Sufi tale, this father eventually locked her up, to no avail. Enraged by her devotion to meditation, he ordered her to be killed. But instead she was saved by a tiger and ultimately became a bodhisattva, an enlightened being who chooses to delay being a Buddha until the whole world has become holy. As Kuan Yin, saint of universal mercy, her compassion extended to all living creatures, even her father. She returned home to save him, to reveal to him his own spark of goodness.

In both these latter tales, the rebellious daughters remain central and triumphant, even with their fathers still alive, whereas in *King Lear*, even though she is the catalyst for the play's action, Cordelia is never as personally powerful or effective as most of the other characters. Why the Cordelia of the British Isles must die with her father while the Sufi princess teaches her father and the Chinese Kuan Yin heals her father may or may not be a question of culture, but it is puzzling that these two ancient patriarchal societies, not renowned for equal rights for women, should allow the daughter to evolve beyond the consciousness of the father whereas the more liberal monarchy punishes her unto death. Does this suggest an earlier time before patriarchy was institutionalized or when it was flowering so fully that storytellers, probably male, could risk using their assertion of the wiser, more flexible daughter as a teaching about a more spiritual consciousness? A beatitude tale? Was Shakespeare anticipating the decline of patriarchy in his tragedy? He was, after all, writing during the reign of Queen Elizabeth.

Perhaps these are three different versions of the very same story, shaped by different tellers within different contexts for different purposes. In all three the story of the daughter is integral to the story of the parent. She carries her lineage into a new world.

PART ONE: STINGER

"Swallow in the dusk...
Spare my little
buzzing friends
among the flowers."

—Basho

To Become or Not to Become

The child's face fell into a frown as she held up her purple section of litmus paper. The papers of her two classmates were turning red. Hers was darkening into blue. Corey had randomly selected her to demonstrate the base. The child expected red like everybody else.

"Try this," Corey said, handing her another strip and holding out Vial B, which contained the acid. Carefully the child dipped the paper in; cautiously she waited until it too turned red. Then with a slight smile of satisfaction she returned to her desk.

Random selection, mused Corey, might not be the way to go on this experiment. Might be better to let kids self-select exceptions to the rule. Warn them ahead of time so they'll feel special and not like odd balls? Would that rob them of the discovery? She was still adjusting her curriculum to these younger students, still startled by their candor.

That obvious disappointment on the child's face nagged at her. During recess Sally cornered her in the hall and whispered, "Did you take the test?"

Corey nodded. "Negative." They high-fived each other, then Sally ran to catch up with her pupils before they paraded past the principal's office. As the grin faded from her face, Corey caught her reflection in a display case. Superimposed upon the faces of the fathers of our country was a frown of her own making—not unlike the disappointment on the child's face when her litmus paper turned blue.

Am I disappointed not to be pregnant, she thought? She'd felt such obvious relief last night when she dipped the white plastic wand stick into her urine stream and the red blinked negative. Stop light. She wasn't ready to let Steve go bouncing out of her life as easily as he'd bounced into it. His departure was inevitable, of course, but for the time being she enjoyed his company, his warmth in her bed, the comfort of being a couple. But, she and Sally agreed, pregnancy would send him scooting out of there faster than a speeding bullet. And Corey had resolved never to have another abortion. She shuddered, remembering that awful first time when she was barely past being a child herself.

That night in her apartment, after a strenuous game of tennis with Steve before he went off to his night class, Corey pulled out a legal sized piece of paper and drew a line down the middle of it. Side A she labeled PRO and Side B she labeled CON.

It was easier to think of CONS: "financial burden—lifelong responsibility— bye-bye Mr. American Pie—trouble with Sally?—my temper—possible child neglect or abuse—repeating dysfunctional family pattern—other opportunities lost (professional advancement, adventures, travel)—loss of freedom—the parent trap—becoming my own mother—having a baby late in life and, like my parents, dying early."

Under PROS she wrote: "I like children, I wouldn't mind one of my own, one to hold onto (at least for awhile) instead of letting go every year—companionship, family, comfort for old age—fitting into the crowd, being just as good as other women, not an old maid—an adventure in itself, time for a change—perpetuation of the species (such as it is)—extending the family line (such as it was)—taking advantage of the opportunity women have of giving birth."

Reflecting on the cons, she realized she was most afraid of losing Sally's friendship. She'd shared Sally's own ambivalence these past few years, when Sally's biological clock was, as they say, ticking. She'd supported Sally's choice in the face of pressure from family, friends and fellow workers to be just like them, married with children. Together they didn't feel left out of the commonplace.

Sally was terrified of giving birth. They decided she must've died of childbirth in some past life. Corey herself was rather intrigued by the prospect—she'd seen kittens, puppies and calves born; even when breached, birth seemed quite natural. Until she realized Sally's resistance ran deeper, Corey'd even contemplated having a baby and giving it to Sally to raise. Since Sally came from such a happy family, a veritable bower of bliss compared to Corey's own, this resistance surprised Corey. Still it made a bond between them. But Sally was married and she was not. Sally had family and, now that Gram was dead and Clare had moved to Florida, Corey did not.

Reflecting on the PROS, she realized the strongest pull was toward a sense of family of her own. Ever since Gram had died last fall, Corey had felt lonelier than ever. Homesick even. She'd all but lost touch with Jack and Bruce and their families and felt no great desire to reconnect. But she missed Gram, Mom, Daddy and John. It hadn't been the greatest family, despite all their pretense, and it sure was a mess at the end, but it had been better than nothing. And nothing was what she faced when she looked at her future.

Which didn't mean, of course, that having a child was the answer. Maybe she was just bored, anticipating a midlife crisis, ready to dip her prospects in some change agent and see what might turn up. Sally was pressuring her to become the principal, but Corey wasn't taking that personally. They were both just so sick and tired of that amateur fascist who'd been running the school into the ground for the past few years. Corey herself still toyed with the idea of being an exchange teacher in Africa or Asia. She was ripe for some real adventure, the adventure she should've had when she was younger, when she was so busy establishing herself as normal after her own personal experience of the dramatic decline of family values.

Mom and Gram, she bet, never even thought about whether or not to have children. Gram probably didn't have much choice, not being the spinster type. Mom did everything without apparently questioning why, just for the challenge of it. But Corey herself seemed doomed to question every move. Perhaps because her generation of women was the first who really had a choice, tenuous though it was.

Hearing Steve at the door she put away her tally sheet, preparing to greet him and listen to him tell about his class. *What makes me think I could raise a child all by myself?* she wondered as she smiled at him. *What can I be thinking?*

That night as she lay in bed soothed by his deep breathing, she continued to mull over this choice. Her time was running out. Of all the thousands of eggs in her body, you'd think one of them might have gotten impregnated by now. Until AIDS she wasn't that vigilant about protection. You'd think at least one of those eggs would stand up and demand some attention.

Female scientists, she thought, are discovering, apparently, that eggs are not passive receptors of male aggression as traditionally assumed. Those little sperm are confused and lost, squeamish about actual contact. It's the magnetism of the egg which pulls them toward conception.

She guessed her eggs weren't magnetic enough. It's as if her biology echoed her other ambivalences. Or maybe she was infertile. Of course she'd never checked that out. What was the point of knowing?

*   *   *   *

That night she dreamt she'd given birth to a litter of babies. There must have been at least six of them. As soon as they were born, nurses started carrying them away from her—off in different directions. She cried out for them, to no avail. It seems they were going to be put up for adoption, without her permission.

She woke up passionately wanting to have those children back. Funny how the scale tips. All this time she'd been resisting, then suddenly she couldn't wait to give birth. Those reproductive hormones must kick in something fierce, she thought, the closer you get to the deadline. She'd heard of women having babies into their forties, but she knew if she didn't do it before she was forty, she never would. It was in her blood to have them when you're young and healthy. What else was in her blood worried her. The nutty family.

And yet Gram and Mom were both remarkable. Part of her wouldn't mind carrying on that matrilineage, as long as she didn't have to become a queen bee like her mother. Or a fool like her grandmother.

She recalled an African statue she'd seen at the Smithsonian last time she'd taken her class there on a field trip. It had three layers, like a totem pole. On the bottom was a woman with a baby at her breast, nursing, a baby on her back, hanging in a pouch, and two toddlers in front of each of her feet; on the second layer was a replica of the woman on the bottom, with her own four children; and at the top was a replica of the other two women, with her own family group. Corey wondered if the bottom woman was the grandmother or the granddaughter, whether the statue reversed the patriarchal hierarchy. What struck Corey most was the obvious grin on the face of the woman on top as she gazed down upon the infant at her breast. What a contrast to the dismay on Corey's face as she contemplated a similar prospect.

It's too late for me to repeat the exact pattern, she thought, to have four children like Mom did or seven, like Gram did. What scared her was she'd end up reproducing the same family her mother had produced, but that was impossible. Chaos theory told her that. But systems theory warned her to watch out. It was naive to think you could avoid the pattern you inherited, even if it played itself out in different ways. Her nephews and nieces were chips off the old block. Her own apple, in some ways, hadn't fallen far from the tree. Of course, if you chose carbon copies or negative images of family members, like Jack and Bruce did, then history was bound to repeat itself.

The key was to mate with a different strain, something foreign, something unlike anything the Chance Family had ever seen. John tried that, but there wasn't time for the difference to take root. Maybe she should adopt. That would bypass the genetic code. But it wouldn't necessarily produce a different kind of family. Pieces of any shape, size or color could still be made to fit into the existing puzzle.

She knew she was not an anomaly like her brother John or a mutant like her mother Bea. Her only hope of breaking the genetic code was that she was lucky enough to be born female in late 20th Century America.

Given how dysfunctional her own family had been, it wasn't surprising she'd waited this long to deal with this issue of continuity. She realized now with some dread that if she hoped to avoid repeating the worst of the family pattern, she'd have to understand her particular family system better than she did.

Trouble was, last time her family was together, they were splitting apart. That moment was frozen in her memory. She thought she'd handled it at the time, when she was seeing Marion. But that must've been grief therapy, not healing for life. Nothing had happened since then to cause within Corey a paradigm shift. Not even Gram's death or Clare's move—simply more losses, more reason to shut herself off from the past.

The family disintegration began around the time of her mother's retirement. Corey decided that before another pregnancy scare, she'd better revisit that time. So she dug out an old journal she'd kept when she was in therapy and, reluctantly at first, wrote in it on evenings when Steve was in class.

Corey's Journal

LOOKING BACK

When Mom said she wanted to retire, I had no idea what it might trigger. Actually, her announcement embarrassed me. I knew she didn't just mean she was going to quit her job—not retiring in that sense. No, it was bound to mean a show, something grandiose. She could never just quietly do something, that wasn't her style. There had to be the obligatory bash.

I was in my twenties and still wanted my mother to be like everybody else's mother. I didn't want to tell my friends why I was going home. Their mothers would never retire. Some of them never had jobs in the first place; others just quit. Most of them would probably be doing the same work at home or on the job until the day they died.

An anniversary party or something like that everyone would have understood, but Mom and Dad never made it to their fortieth. Hell, she was only in her fifties—fifty-five?—when she decided to retire. I knew she needed a change, after Dad died. She acted, for the first time in her life, weary. Her health seemed ok, her cholesterol wasn't too high, she already hated eggs so she just had to cut out butter (a symbol of wealth to her, she once confided) and red meat (which I think she felt made her one of the boys).

She told me privately she was tired of holding it all together. Her siblings, her employees, us—she had been taking care of people most of her life. I backed her on that—I wasn't sure at the time her holding everything together was so good for the rest of us. That was before I saw how totally everything fell apart when she stopped.

I wasn't sure, though, she'd be able to stop. I figured she'd be like those boxers who keep coming out of retirement to fight one more fight. Could she really settle for being Moses, watching from the mountain (or wherever Moses was when they told him he couldn't go the rest of the way)? Maybe at the time Mom hadn't planned to disappear. Maybe she imagined still managing, 'consulting,' from a distance.

I'm still not sure why she did it. I'm pretty sure she didn't anticipate what actually happened. But what did she hope would happen? I just don't know. But I can imagine. I can hear her saying to herself (as she was then, not as she was later):

"I wouldn't mind somebody caring for me while I'm still in my prime, before I get so damn doddering dependent someone *has* to take care of me and resents it. I'd rather die first than be cared for like that, grudgingly, dutifully.

"Time to sit back in my easy chair and let them come to me, wait on me for a change. Let them lavish me with gifts. Let them entertain me, challenge me, educate me. (Fat chance.) Time to dream, sniff the flowers, listen to music, watch the sunset—all that stuff. Time to head out in a new direction before it's too late—a trip to the Andes, an African safari, sailing to Tahiti."

See? Nothing halfway about her, nothing retiring or reticent or held-back. How I ever turned out to be her daughter, I'll never know.

I can hear her voice now, summing up her life: "I sure wasn't Superwoman, but I did a great job balancing family and business. When the kids got rowdy, I stuck 'em in the stockroom for the summer so they could see what it might be like to have that kind of job the rest of their lives. When the employees got alienated, I invited them to a family picnic so they could see what fun it is to play together as well as work together.

"The American Dream…lots of women now are trying for it—though I can't see putting a kid in daycare at the age of three months. I was sort of a pioneer, even before women's lib."

She was a rare bird in the fifties, ready to go in the sixties, and by the time she was looking back in the eighties, women were pouring into what were traditionally men's jobs. Of course that was before the economy started collapsing and they were stuck supporting families at home *and* on the job. But to tell the truth, I'm not sure, now that I'm less personally invested, she had much use for women.

*   *   *   *

I guess, looking back on it now, the scene that stands out, for some reason, is when I drove out to the cabin to find Mom, to tell her about John. I still can't believe I didn't realize he had AIDS. How could I be so naive? I remember puzzling over the way the nurse said to me as I was leaving, "Don't worry, pneumonia usually isn't fatal these days." I was shocked; of course it isn't fatal, I thought. People even walk around with full-blown cases. It makes sense I'd keep replaying that denial. What I still can't understand is why the scene at the cabin keeps nagging me.

The sun was setting when I got there. I'd forgotten how long, bumpy and windy that dirt road was. Dark tree trunks and their shadows sliced up the golden light into rays which faded before I reached the cabin. Except for one light in a back room, the cabin was dark. I heard muffled sounds in the woods. I knocked. No answer.

From the darkness of the woods I heard two voices call my name, Clare's and Mom's. I was surprised they'd be out there walking in the dark. I held myself stiff until Mom stepped up on the porch. She reached out to me, not in that grand manner she sometimes had, but shyly, tentatively. My response was just as tentative. But then she hugged me fully, not the usual push-pull where it feels like she's holding you off, keeping her distance, while she's embracing you.

Suddenly, I pulled back, as if I were drowning. I don't know why. I felt as if I were hugging a stranger. Someone I didn't know any more than I know the Queen of the Nile. Someone who didn't know me any better than Cleopatra would. Anyway, the front door opened, Gram stood there looking sleepy, I told them about John being in the hospital, there was a bustle of activity. While I waited for them to get ready, I felt relief that Mom hadn't jumped down my throat, as only she can. Then we were off, the whole crew. That's about it.

Why do I keep replaying this scene? Guilt that I couldn't respond to her as fully as she obviously wanted? Maybe. In retrospect, of course, that seems even more of a shame.

Or am I holding on for positive reasons? Maybe. It was a rare time when she wanted to be close to me. But I didn't feel good about it then, and now I recall it with dread.

What do I wish had happened instead? Oh, I don't know. I don't even want to think about it.

Now that I've chosen to explore the past, I can't help thinking about it. About them. They won't let me forget again. The voices suddenly won't shut up. All those separate voices talking at once. All that noise in my head.

DIALOGUE

───────────── ▼ ─────────────

This novel is what some call an "oppositional narrative." It not only transports an old story into modern times, it switches gender in the process. Instead of King Lear, we have "Queen" Bea. Instead of three daughters, we have three sons and one daughter, with the youngest daughter and son serving as an androgynous counter to the queenly power.

Why do this? Simply imagining a gender switch can tell us a great deal about our attitudes about gender. When I've asked American college-age composition students to picture waking up and looking into the mirror to discover they had, overnight, switched gender, the girls for the most part were delighted and the boys were horrified.

The phrase "Queen Bea" suggests a similar alteration. A "Queen Bee" is considered a pampered darling, a bossy type whose rulings are often whimsical or arbitrary. A king's position is not so initially in question; his authority is not automatically challenged. As linguistic scholars have pointed out, as soon as a woman assumes a name or a role, its connotation becomes degraded (Miller and Swift, *Words and Women*).

> "Does the Queen try to sound like the King, imitating his tone, his inflections, his phrasing, his point of view? Or does she 'talk back' to him in her own vocabulary, her own timbre, insisting on her own viewpoint?" (Gilbert and Gubar, *The Madwoman in the Attic*)

In other words, she's damned if she does and damned if she doesn't. If she imitates the king, she lacks authenticity. If she talks her own talk, she lacks authority.

> The writer of an "oppositional narrative," according to Alice Ostriker, "deconstructs a prior myth or story and constructs a new one which includes, instead of excluding, herself...[This project is] fraught with some irony since one of the social functions of mythic narratives is precisely the solidification, consolidation, and affirmation of a hegemony." ("The Thieves of Language," *Signs* 8:1, 72)

The irony emerges from the fact that most of us are allied with both past and future, our own lives mediating between them. *King Lear* is one of my favorite pieces of literature, with its assertion of spiritual values over material, love over power. I'm not the only writer who has played with its tale. Jane Smiley's novel, *A Thousand Acres* transposes Lear to contemporary America. The 1990 Mabou Mines production of Lear, directed by Lee Breuer, featured a woman in the title role: "not as a man but as a classic mother figure confronting what the director"—a man—"believes is the crucial issue facing women today: can they have love and power at the same time?" (*New York Times*)

I venture to bend the narrative to a different purpose. But I dialogue with Shakespeare knowing that I have as much right to take liberties with my source as he did with his.

> "The act of looking back, of seeing with fresh eyes, of entering an old text from a new critical direction," Adrienne Rich reminds us, "is an act of survival. Until we understand the assumptions in which we are drenched, we cannot know ourselves...We need to know the writing of the past and know it differently than we have ever known it: not to pass on a tradition but to break its hold on us." ("When We Dead Awaken: Writing as Revision," *Lies, Secrets and Silence*, 35)

The fresh eyes I bring to this narrative are not just the mother's, not just the daughter's, but the whole family's. The systems view is multi-faceted, with a different point of view for each face of the whole. But the perspective I bring as narrator is also an *other* side of the dialogue begun by some unknown storyteller ages ago and continued by Shakespeare not so very long ago. The storyteller's is the ultimate power in any narrative.

> "This 'narrative displacement,' displacing the attention to the other side of the story, is like breaking the sentence because it [gives] voice to the muted. Displacement is a committed identification with Otherness," Rachel DuPlessis tells us. "A change of point of view reveals the implicit politics of narrative: the choice of the teller or the perspective will alter the core assumptions and one's sense of the tale. By putting the female eye, ego, and voice at the center of the tale, displacement asks the kinds of questions that certain feminist historians have, in persistent ways, put forth: How do events, selves and grids for understanding look when viewed by a female subject, evaluated in ways she chooses?" (*Writing Beyond the Ending*, 108–109)

But ultimately this particular narrative is not oppositional but exploratory, not so much about gender as about humanity. When we include women not just as narrators but also as heroes, we expand our notion of what is human. I'm not trying to show that women are immune to power abuses or that they would rule differently than men have. My narrative strategy is more about describing a fuller spectrum of our experiences of individual power, power sharing, and loss of power, of what authority is and how it is won, of how the dynamics of hierarchy, command and control in the whole system affect all of us, and how to pass on to the next generation our compassion and wisdom as well as our possessions and positions.

PART TWO: THE QUEEN

"In the woman's meditation the Self appeared as a deer, which said to the ego, 'I am your child and your mother. They call me the connecting animal because I connect people, animals, and even stones with one another if I enter them. I am your fate, or the 'objective I...' When I appear, I redeem you from the meaningless hazards of life. The fire burning inside me burns in the whole of nature. If a [person] loses it, [she] becomes egocentric, lonely, disoriented and weak.

—Marie-Louise Von Franz

BEA
Head of Harmony Enterprises, widow of Jack, mother of
Dick, Bruce, Corey and John, daughter of Mildred, called The Queen

RETIREMENT

Down the dark hallway, which led from the showroom to Bea's office, Clare followed Bea. As usual she had to rush to keep up with Bea's long, bold stride. While passing the switch, Bea flipped it up and the lights above, one after the other, flickered on before them like some heavenly spotlight.

Aging just makes her more handsome, thought Clare, as Bea glanced sideways at herself in the hall mirror, running her fingers through her naturally frosted hair. Even though Bea automatically sucked her tummy in as she passed the mirror, she'd kept her trim figure into her fifties.

Why, thought Clare, has age melted me while it's only crystallized Bea? The gleam in Bea's eye was as sharp as ever while the glow in Clare's softened every day. Without the challenge and structure of this job, Clare thought, I'll just dissolve into a puddle. Isn't there some way I can change her mind?

In Bea's office the light was subdued, sunlight through a corner of picture windows fading into dusk. Bea collapsed into her plush executive desk chair and rotated away from the computer—always on—so she could lean on the desk, her chin resting in her right hand as the fingers of her left hand tapped on the blotter.

Clare sank into the armchair facing the desk and prepared to listen. This time of day, after the employees had gone home, was when Bea was most likely to switch to the confidential tone reserved especially for Clare, who was not only her next in command but also her old friend.

"What worries me, Clare, is the party. Of course I'm not calling it a birthday party, but can I trick fate? My birthdays have always been jinxed."

"Always?" Clare looked up from the low chair, positioned so that its occupant had to look up at the person behind the desk. AS CEO of Harmony Enterprises, a small company which she founded and still ran, Bea knew very well how to overcome the many prejudices against women in positions of power. She ignored the insults—Bitch, Harpy, Ball-Buster—and she didn't mind the complementary titles, like Queen, albeit grudging, envious, or ironic.

"First one I remember I was three. We couldn't afford a cake, so Mama put three candles on a big cookie. Of course the candles melted all over the cookie, icing it with wax. I didn't know at the time that things could get a whole lot worse, so I cried. Spoiled everything."

"Probably the last time you ever cried." This softer side of Bea was one she showed only to Clare. So even though this complaint was all too familiar, Clare settled into that comforting and flattering sense of being special these confidences usually engendered within her.

"Yeah. Then there was the year Jason got his finger caught in the toaster. They were afraid they might have to amputate. Instead they dismantled the toaster. That was the end of that party."

"Never a dull moment in that housefull." How many tales Clare had heard of Bea's chaotic family? Who would ever guess this sophisticated women with her distinguished carriage and tasteful power suits would have risen from such messy roots?

"Then there was the year the candles set the curtains on fire. Oh, the disasters just go on and on. I can smile about it now, but when you're a kid…" Bea sighed.

"Birthdays are pretty important—make you feel special." How many times had they played this duet, variations on this theme?

"One time really sticks under my skin. I don't know how old I was but I was feeling pretty perky despite everything. Uncle Sammy started teasing me. At least that's what Mama called it. He said I was 'full of myself' and 'too uppity.' He said I must think I was 'the cat's meow,' or is it 'the cat's pajamas'? He said it with that dumb grin of his, but I could feel the bite. It confused me. What had I done to bother him? Did he resent the attention I was getting? Heck, your birthday's the only time anyone does pay any attention to you."

"Mine's right after Christmas—they didn't pay much attention to me then."

"But you were the baby—you got plenty of attention the rest of the time."

"Yeah, I guess." Clare resented this standard dismissal of her own childhood, which hadn't exactly been a bower of bliss although it certainly couldn't compete with Bea's woes.

"So of course I sassed him back and then he really got mean. 'You little snot,' and 'Aren't we stuck up?' and 'You asking for trouble?' (Having dealt with Dad, I knew what 'asking for trouble' meant, so I decided not to ask for any.) Another birthday down the drain." Bea's fingers stopped drumming as she tried to smooth out a crease in the blotter.

"I felt just like a balloon he'd stuck a pin into. Maybe I was all puffed up, full of life. But the way he poked at me made me feel all dirty inside, just full of hot air. When that happens, you sorta collapse from the inside with a little sigh. The next thing you know, you're lying on the floor all shriveled and ugly, with a gash in your side and your next stop, the trash. You ever feel like that?"

"Yeah, sure, I know what you mean." Actually, now that Clare had been told Bea would be announcing her retirement at the party, she was afraid deflation would be just around the corner for both of them. She herself did not want to retire, but she couldn't imagine stepping into Bea's shoes, even though, if truth be known, she was the one who ran the company on a day-to-day basis. "But you must've had at least one good birthday. I remember your mom telling me…"

"Not when I was growing up. During the war, it wasn't just having no money that squeezed the birthdays into nothing. Mama was all bent out of shape worrying about Dad. She expected a telegram any day saying he'd been blown to smithereens. After the war he came back all in one piece, but shattered inside, I guess. He didn't talk about it.

"My birthday that year he was so drunk he knocked over the cupcakes. She'd only gotten one package: "for the kids only." (Maybe that's what made him so mad; he couldn't have a cupcake.) Of course they all landed on the soft icing part and stuck on the floor. I started screaming and Mama slapped me—in front of my friends. For the first and only time in my life I lit into her like a windmill on a rampage. That was the end of that party."

"You sure you want to have a party?" Clare hesitated to ask again, you sure you want to retire? They'd been over that so many times, Bea was adamant. "You got me convinced they *are* jinxed. Or does that just make you want to break the jinx?"

"Yeah, it does, but I probably should let it be." Bea turned to the keyboard on her right and played a familiar song, a tune her son John had composed. Then she pushed a few buttons on the keyboard, swiveled over to the computer, made some adjustments there, listened as the song emerged from the computer fully orchestrated. She shook her head, not yet pleased with the result. Turning back to her audience, she gave Clare a wry smile.

"My last party as a 'child' I'll never forget. I must've been about fifteen. Mama was in the hospital—having another baby or getting repairs from having so many babies, I don't remember—and Dad forgot it was my birthday. No surprise there, but I had a habit of sulking on my birthdays—I guess my feelings were hurt—and this irked him."

Then, as if talking to herself, she murmured, "A nice man I called Daddy when I was little would toss the ball with us, carry us on his shoulders, show us how to catch fireflies. Mama says he was the same as Dad. But he changed—that was before the war. It was the war that changed him, Mama says, but I remember. The war just made him worse. He'd already changed."

Clare listened more intently. These revelations were something new, closer to the bone. But they quickly gave way to the old story, albeit one of Clare's favorites.

"Anyway, he took out his belt and, the buckle end loose, started swinging at me. Usually when he got mean like that, we ran away or Mama stood between us and caught the blows. And usually he was so tanked up by then, he'd fall down swinging. But Mama wasn't there and I was too big to run away."

"So what'd you do?" Clare asked, the perfect foil.

"I glared at him. He pulled back his arm. The buckle gleamed under the light like snake's teeth ready to bite. I could see those fangs sinking into my back if I ran, into my face if I stood my ground. Then suddenly something in me started to hiss. I was as tall as he was by then. And a whole lot steadier on my feet."

"'Go ahead and beat me with that belt,' I said to him. 'But if you do, you'll never have another night's rest. I swear I'll get you. Somehow, sometime, when you least expect it. So if you beat me, make sure you do a good job. Finish me off now. Because if you don't, your life won't be worth a plug nickel.'"

"Well, now, that's impressive." Clare knew only too well what Bea could do in the resistance department.

"It just came out like that: full blown, well-rehearsed—the words I must have wanted to put into Mama's mouth every time he lit into her.

"He glared at me. Eye to eye. Suddenly I was an opponent, no longer just a victim. Then he lowered that belt down and stared at me until I walked off, turning my back to him. That moment my life changed forever. He never threatened me again. In fact, he never spoke to me again. Within a month he was gone."

Again Bea fell to murmuring. Clare strained to listen. It was as if a more somber, more authentic instrument had joined the orchestration. Perhaps the hope of retirement was providing a chink in Bea's armor. Perhaps leaving this job and all its real and false power would be for her the opening to a softer self. But what would it mean for Clare?

"Mama at home recuperating, him without a job, me trying to hold it all together...he never shows up one day after heading off to look for a job (usually ended up at the tavern).

"Was it my fault? Mama was so upset, I blamed myself. Later I figured Good Riddance. We were better off without him. Mama never did know what happened. Maybe he didn't come back because he tried that belt trick on someone not as soft as me. No one's ever pushed me around since then.

"You can be sure I shopped around before I married Jack. Maybe not the most exciting person in the world, but steady as a rock. Always could depend on him. Always provided for his family. Never put me down, jeered at me, threatened punishment if I didn't do what he wanted me to do. Wasn't going to repeat Mama's mistake: your husband's your biggest burden. Made sure, even with Jack, that I could make a go of it on my own—at the drop of a hat or disappearance of an overcoat."

Bea twisted her chair away from Clare, away from the computer, away from the keyboard and sat staring out the windows. Outside the world had turned blue. They sat in silence for a long time.

"What you thinking?" Clare finally dared to ask.

"I haven't celebrated my birthday for years. Most people don't even know when it is. I've accepted the jinx."

Again the murmur: "Convenient now that years leap by while I creep beside them. Figured it was my birth that was cursed. Way Mom tells it, I was out and running before they'd even cut the cord. That's the way she wants it to be. Her story's that I never wanted to be a child, so I grew up faster than a blink of her eye. Shit, no one ever asked me. Her eye was always fixed on the newest child. She could've spent my childhood blinking and never seen me—except as her right-hand helper.

"Were they even married when she got pregnant? Isn't her turning all my birthdays into disasters a way of saying they didn't want me? If so, she'd never admit it. The other kids had decent birthdays: if we had enough money, if Dad wasn't drunk, if there wasn't some natural disaster occurring at the time. Thanks to me."

This dark strain in Bea was beginning to worry Clare. It was time to cheer her up. "Well, you sure saw to it that your own kids had birthday celebrations to beat the band."

"My younger sisters and brothers too."

"So now it's your turn."

Bea rotated back to face Clare. In the darkening light her face looked surprisingly vulnerable. This directness of emotion was startling to someone like Clare, so adept at reading between the edges for signs of tenderness.

Bea screwed up her face. "But I've got such a queasy feeling about it. Will Uncle Sammy rise up from his grave to make fun of me? Will one of the kids get stuck in a manhole? Will Dad show up drunk? Will one of the guests collapse?"

"Hey, don't worry. Your birthday's a blessing, not a curse."

"Yeah, maybe, but do me a favor—don't tell anybody it's my birthday. If I don't expect any presents, I might not get any grief either."

SEPARATION

Fat chance, Bea thought, this is going to be any fun. She was dressed to the teeth as she joined Pearl, her oldest if not dearest friend, at the Captain's Table. They were on a cruise together. For Bea it was an escape; for Pearl, an adventure.

While Pearl charmed the captain and his guests, Bea retreated into the menu. Pate, filet of sole, blackberry yogurt soup, breast of goose, piccata a la Milanese, fried Camembert. We're already stuffed, Bea thought. Stuck at this table full of strangers. What boring conversation: the service, the ship, the weather, other voyages, absolutely nothing about our real lives, jobs, families. *A life of luxury is not for me*, Bea thought. *I can't stand doing nothing day after day. If anybody thinks I'm actually going to retire at my age, they sure don't know me. I've got to quit the company to move on to something bigger and better. I hope that offer from Stevens comes through, that he wasn't just trying to swing a deal. But if it doesn't*, she thought, *I'll find something else. My resume is first rate and my contacts, even better.*

The more Pearl shone, the more Bea glowered. *No, Pearl, I don't want to finish your banana split!*

Funny how everyone buzzes around me first, then settles down with Pearl, Bea thought. *Clare might point out, in her own quiet way, how they're shying away from my sharp edges. The rounder and softer Pearl gets, the more accessible she seems, absorbing everything, revealing nothing.*

Bea missed Clare. Being with Pearl was a disappointment. This was more time than they'd spent together in years and they seemed to have nothing to say to each other.

All we do, Bea thought, *is sit on the top deck staring out at the empty rim of ocean. Much as I tried to get her talking this afternoon, she would have none of it. At least I finally said what was on my mind.* "I've never given my children any reason for shame. I thought they were proud of me. I feel betrayed."

When Bea said this, Pearl seemed to wince. But other than that Bea wasn't sure she'd heard her. Maybe the sound of the ship splashing through the waves had drowned her voice.

Finally Pearl responded. "It's hard not to feel betrayed sometimes." Bea wondered why Pearl said that. Pearl's daughters gave her no trouble, none Bea knew about. Opal was quite a flirt, Ruby's clothes were far from smart, but neither's given Pearl a moment's real worry. "But children can shame us without meaning to," Pearl added.

What's she mean by that? Bea thought. Shame? Don't I know about shame? Don't echo shame to me, Pearl. *My good-for-nothing father, shabby mother, too large family, threadbare clothes—my whole childhood eroded by shame. And shame about shame—Mom who gave so much. How could I be ashamed just because she dressed so dowdy and spoke so wrong and couldn't make it financially? It's not so great to feel so lousy about your roots, especially once you've gotten free of the squalor. Tried to polish Mom up—didn't work, though she took to school like...a dolphin in this sea.*

Bea pulled herself out of her internal whirlpool and spoke. "Good mothers, they say, produce selfish children. I've obviously cared too much for mine."

"We sacrifice ourselves for our children, I guess, because we have no choice," Pearl murmured.

"But somehow I had the illusion they would at least learn some generosity from our example."

Pearl shrugged. Bea wondered how she could get her to open up. She didn't want to pry, she just wanted to talk with her. Tell her about it all.

Corey might die, the doctor said, so I kept vigil every night till the fever broke. How many days was I late to work waiting for John to stop screaming and go into school by himself?

"Is this why we have children," Bea muttered, "to learn first hand the sting of ingratitude?"

All Pearl did at that point was sigh.

Even though Pearl had resisted the conversation, Bea thought as espresso was served, *I just couldn't stop talking, damn it. Why didn't I just shut up? My anger just welled up.*

"I could've shaken Corey, sitting there so dumb, with that tight little, smug little expression," Bea had said.

Pearl's face tightened. *Why?* Bea thought. *Did she feel sorry for Corey? Oh Christ!*

"Her father spoiled her rotten." Bea tried to evoke some common ground— Pearl's father sure didn't spoil her rotten. "And the way John kept shrinking back into himself—how does he come off being so goddam tender?"

Lord Almighty, Bea recalled now, then Pearl shrank back into herself—*I missed it then, but I can see it now.*

Damn, damn, damn.

It was all I could do not to rush over and smash their smug heads together, like eggshells. Or choke those smirks off their silly faces.

Finally she realized she might as well say nothing. Pearl had clamed up. *Why does she have to take everything so personally?* Bea thought. *Is she wallowing in her own doldrums? Or is she just hard of hearing? She never was much of a listener.*

Retreat, Bea thought with an internal groan. *Why do I feel so drained? Some birthday jinx—a deathblow this time? Why didn't they just spit in my face before the party? No, stab me in the back—where the heart hides.*

Then while the dinner guests turned to face the band for some old favorites, Bea became even more lost in thought.

All those years I cared for you, fed you, clothed you, changed your diapers, washed your clothes, mended the rips and sewed on the missing buttons, potty trained you, replaced the zippers and patched the holes, washed the snot from your noses and cut your hair and showed you how to care for your nails and minded your manners and humored your tastes and peeves and bought you treats and surprises and whatever you asked for as soon as we could afford it and tolerated your friends and listened to your stories and praised your efforts and couched my advice in flattering tones and treated your sores and took you to doctors and drove you back and forth to lessons and dances and parties and sports events and paid for your schooling and lent you my car and paid for your insurance and cried with you and worried over you and kissed you and hugged you and let you go when you were ready and let you come home when you had to and so on and so on and so on and so on.

And what did I ever charge you for all this? Nothing!

Years of investment of time, money, and love and what do I get in return? What do I have to show for it? What comes back to me?

Nothing, nothing, nothing, nothing.

So now that's all you'll get from me. The business you can have (once you're ready to assume responsibility), but your mother is like this empty ocean—with nothing left to give.

*   *   *   *

From the way she strode confidently into the lounge, no one would have ever guessed Bea was uneasy. She'd never been out alone in a place like this. Jack had always been with her.

Why'd I let Pearl talk me into coming here tonight? she thought. *Never had much time to sit around in bars—always hated them, where Daddy spent my childhood.*

She found a table back in a corner where she could see in every direction and looked around for Pearl. Finally she spotted her with her new boyfriend in an even darker corner. Shoulda known Pearl would be off flirting—that's why she wanted to come on this cruise. *How she could be enamored of that guy is beyond me—handsome yes, but shallow as all get out, and judging from the untanned part of his finger, recently married. Recently divorced, Pearl tells me—I bet.*

A slight, rather fey waiter arrived to take her order.

So what'll I do now? she thought. *Just sit here drinking, watching them dance? Guess it beats sitting alone in the stateroom.*

Oops, she thought, looking away, *that old guy is eyeing me. Looks a little like Mr. Tuttle, my eighth grade science teacher—grey hair, mustache, weak chin, bulbous nose. He must be—about my age, that's a shock—makes me an old gal. Wonder what he sees in me? I don't see much in him.*

The waiter brought Bea her scotch on the rocks and asked if she'd like anything to eat. She made a face at the thought of any more food. He winced and became haughty. *This waiter, she thought, is so wispy, supercilious—cut from the same shifty cloth as John (not to be trusted). Let's try growling and see what happens.* She pointed out the spill on her napkin and ordered another one. *Yep—he prims up—still wispy, but more respectful.*

John's gone, Jack's gone, she thought, *they've all abandoned me. Mama always said men couldn't be trusted. I thought I'd proven her wrong—with my four splendid men, so unlike my father, my brothers. At least I still have Dick, my lifesaver. I don't know what I'd do without him now that Jack's gone. I keep forgetting to tell him that.*

The man with the bulbous nose approached her table. Amazing, she thought, how arrogantly some men will move into your space without a qualm. Even in public places like this, few women I know would barge in this way without at least a request, a warning.

He turned on the charm, but she wasn't impressed. Her armor closed around her. *What does he think I am—a wealthy widow?* she thought. *I've managed, at least, to keep my figure, as so many my age haven't. Despite the battle with the bulge after the hysterectomy.*

Only slightly flattered by this attention and relieved not to be so obviously alone, even though she found him boring, she tolerated him. He sat down at her table and ordered a drink. Then she noticed a bulge in his crotch and her final shield went up. She asked him to leave her alone. He laughed, not believing she meant it.

"Buzz off, buster," she murmured so only he could hear it. She didn't want to shame him. But then, embarrassed, he started to mock her. She couldn't help it. As soon as the jeering tone rose in his voice, she poured her drink into his lap. An apparent accident. His face became contorted. Contemplating revenge, she guessed. The bartender snickered as he exited.

After a decent interval, Bea stood up and waved to Pearl. Pearl didn't see her. She's too lost in lust, Bea thought, deciding not to go over to visit with them. She was hurt they hadn't come over to her. *I better get out of here*, she thought... *That snicker's rising in my ear to a sneer.*

Dad pouring a bottle of beer over my head when I was sassy. It wasn't so much the beer—cold and fizzy funny—but the jeer that hurt. I think Mama knocked the bottle out of his hand—I remember it bouncing against the icebox. She was rewarded with a black eye. That was before the war.

Bea couldn't sleep. The alcohol sitting in her stomach felt like a clogged drain. What was that ringing in her ears—the sound of laughter? Mocking, sneering, jeering, laughter that stabs and tears.

It will not let me be, she thought, clamping her hands over her ears.

Was I too full of myself? Did I ask for this?

I'm afraid I'll go crazy with the sound. Everyone's laughing at me.

The ship shuddered. Bea wondered why. It seemed to be shifting its rudder; a dull thud stretched to a high pitched scream.

They're fighting again. We better lie in wait, hidden beyond the words that snarl and snap at each other. We've heard all this before. We know enough to hide beyond bruising distance and listen with buried ears to the roller coaster ride of her screams, his taunts.

She wrapped the pillow around her head.

The sound under my pillow muffles into rising, falling tones. I can play with the sound, run it round my head. I can turn what rises into falling, what falls into rising. Waves of pain subside, become lullabies. I'm turning the sound around.

It's a kind of magic. I feel powerful. I'm making music. I'm turning coal into gold.

Finally Bea sat up and flopped the pillow into her lap. *I might as well face the fact*, she thought, *that I can't sleep. All night I've lain awake, my strings taut, ready to break.*

She tried humming. No new music came. She felt dried up. She sang old songs.

Someone banged on the wall, shouted for her to "shut up!" She curled up under the covers.

Talk about shrinking into yourself, she thought. *Now I'm tight as a ball, but I can't get small enough.*

She glanced at the clock. It was 5 a.m.. *I guess Pearl isn't coming back here tonight*, she thought as she got up and turned on the light.

*   *   *   *

Bea's Journal

"The ocean stretches out around us, an empty plate. Beneath her calm surface, a wealth of life. She offers us none of it: no port, no sail, no view, no wisp of cloud, much less a glimpse of whale, flash of gull, white cap. Full but empty. Given out, given up, given in…

"I'm tired of talking to myself. So for the sake of sanity I've bought this notebook to write in. We kept journals in college English. Once I looked back over mine and discovered the seeds of my life: the family, the music, the teaching, the business. Maybe out of this will emerge seeds for the next half (?) of my life. Maybe I'll find music again. At least it might keep me from thinking the same horrible thoughts over and over, the proverbial broken records.

"But don't expect anything polished, dear reader. Dear self, I should say, because no one ever read my other journal except myself. Which is good: I can say whatever I want and no one's feeling will be hurt.

"All Pearl wants to talk about these days is Lover Boy. Whatever was bothering her before sure isn't worrying her now. Amazing how easily she can distract herself. Guess it beats moping around, like I'm doing.

"We can't talk about anything real anyway (This *amour* of hers certainly isn't real.) Whenever we start complaining about the kids, we get stuck defending ourselves. Down deep we must be blaming ourselves for being bad mothers. Isn't that why we've got such rotten kids? We go round and round the same vicious cycle. We can't pull each other out of it because we're both in it. (Let me remind myself next time not to go on a cruise with another drowning woman.)"

*   *   *   *

"Keep dreaming about Pearl. The other night she was caught in some giant machine with two curved sides, like a shell. It was closing down on her and she was trapped inside. I tried to hold it open, but it was too strong and it snapped shut. I pulled my fingers out just in time.

"Last night I dreamt all my teeth fell out. They just sat in my mouth like marbles. When I tried to tell Pearl about this, my voice rattled but couldn't speak any words. She didn't understand me. So I spit out the marbles one by one and she tried to catch them. We got hysterical laughing. It felt good, even when I woke up.

"Laughing like that reminded me of when we taught together. She was the substitute, so sometimes she taught my classes. We'd tell stories about the same kids: the little guy who always had something live in his lunchbox; the girl who tried to sneak out of the classroom by crawling on her hands and knees: she ended up in the broom closet. Laughing in those days made the absurdities of teaching bearable, even fun.

"I wanted to tell her about the dreams, but she's too busy mooning around with what'shisface. She sure is romancing it up with a vengeance. Guess she wants to see if she still has what it takes."

*   *   *   *

Oh god, Bea thought as she closed her journal, *why did I make such a fool of myself? It was supposed to be a wonderful party. It was going to be a glorious announcement—expansive, generous. Then I lost my temper and ruined the whole thing.*

Poor John, she groaned, *what'd he do to deserve such a mother? We used to love singing together. Why'd he let Corey push him around like that? What happened to my cherub?*

ISOLATION

Stepping into my house, I knew it was no longer my home. All my things were gone. I was torn between weeping and howling. No one greeted me—no surprise. No one but Cinders with her usual desperate enthusiasm, tail going like a windshield wiper in a torrent. No one there—but a house full of their leavings.

I was stunned. Then began searching for my furniture, my knick-knacks, my clothes. Some furniture was in the garage, some nowhere to be found. Boxes full of my personal belongings were piled in the basement. Did they expect me to keep on sailing and leave them full reign?

I opened one of the boxes and found an old photo album. I plopped myself on a pile of dirty clothes next to a new washer and stared at the pictures: Jack and me horseback riding in Calgary on our honeymoon; holding each of the babies as they arrived, one by one by one by one; us playing golf; Dick in his football uniform; Bruce playing chess on the picnic table; Corey dancing through the sprinkler; John in the sandbox; our last trip together, standing by the Pyramids.

I felt empty. Were these my kids? Was this my husband? Was this me? Odd that short cruise on that vacant ocean should leave me so blank.

I felt like curling into the pile of clothes and taking a nap. Then I heard the back door open and what sounded like adult footsteps. I didn't want to go upstairs. But I didn't want to be caught downstairs either. I waited. No more sound. I felt as wary as I did as a kid, my Dad stumbling around in the other room. Frozen.

I could see them standing up there together, close to each other, Dick stiff in his armor, Jeanne tight in her primness. I could see them waiting, with tentative smiles on their faces, for my response. They'd seized control of my home and were expecting me to be pleased?

They looked so defensive—it was like an invitation—if they wanted me to be powerful, I would be. I filled up with rage, hot and explosive. But at the same time something small, tight like a dried pea hardened inside me. Between the expanding fury and the contracting knot, I couldn't do a thing, I couldn't move. In my mind I watched the Big Me rush to action, restoring order—not even bothering to challenge their new authority, ignoring it as they scattered before me, cringing and penitent. At the same time I tightened into that empty pod, curling into myself, invisible, lost.

Suddenly the big me popped, the little me melted. I faced them blankly, a twinge in my stomach, a lump in my throat.

They were fixed like a photo—their smug expressions, their impeccable clothes, made of expensive fabrics in muted, tasteful colors, their poised figures. In that false intimacy of the perfect couple, they posed together, their eyes veiled. I was shocked. They were carbon copies of Jack and me at that age, on our way up. Realizing that, I knew there was no hope.

I sank back into the dirty laundry like a limp nightie.

Then that mirror in my mind suddenly shattered—as if someone'd just thrown a rock into it. Don't expect me to pick up the pieces, I thought. Who cares if the image in the fragments is us or them? My home is gone. I just don't have the energy to fight my own son to get it back. My fear drained away into the limp and musty clothes. I got up, straightened myself up, and climbed out of the basement. No one was there. What had I heard?

I resolved to leave the house without a word, not even a note. The only way they'd even know I'd been there was that Cinders had gone with me. I was sure they'd say I left in a huff, but that would be the softest huff they ever felt.

Secure in this serenity, I glanced into the living room before exiting the house for good. That damn cream colored couch of Jeanne's spread out across the wall where my antique desk had been. What a phony piece of furniture—promising comfort, intimacy, generosity, class. I spit on it. A tiny wet mark marred its virgin surface. But that would soon fade. I glanced at myself in the wall-length mirror she'd installed above the couch, and winced. Something pathetic in the eyes.

In a daze, unable to leave, I wandered into the kitchen, opening drawers and leaving them open—like a teenager. Most of my things were gone, everything was rearranged—obviously by someone who doesn't cook—you had to walk half way across the room to get a knife. My bread knife—they'd kept that. I snatched it up—one thing I could take with me, wherever I was going.

Suddenly I found myself charging into the living room, plunging the knife into the brocade covering of the couch, stabbing, stabbing, stabbing, hacking, tearing. The edges of the knife weren't sharp, but they ripped away at the material like dull pinking shears. No blood. Not even stuffing. Just foam, which resisted, then crumbled at my slashes. Try resting your trim little asses on this mess!

I don't know how long it took to turn that couch into shreds. They'd know now I'd been there. Could there be any doubt who was home?

I raised the knife triumphantly—then froze at the image in the mirror. Light gleamed from metal. The snake's fangs glittering. The hand held high, the weapon shining.

My father's face, tight, glaring, mean as hell. My face, tight, glaring, mean. The knife fell from my hand, no longer mine.

Cinders followed me out. My only assurance that I wasn't a total maniac.

Thank God they hadn't sold or junked the car. I felt inordinate gratitude when it started right away. I stopped at the bank and closed my account before it was too late. Then I drove here, the cabin. I didn't call Bruce, I didn't ask where Mama is, I didn't call Clare and apologize. What I was left to do these responsible things?

*   *   *   *

For the past few days a little me has moved through a fog that hangs both outside, snaking through the woods, and inside, winding through my mind. This me is functional enough to buy groceries, get the electricity turned on, order firewood, clean out the wood stove. Had I stayed in that house that was my home I might have destroyed it.

That stranger in the photo is my child? Maybe we were that self-assured, but never that prim, that cocky. I wasn't born to the silver spoon; I knew what it took to get that high. But mostly I don't even think about that, all I think about is the next meal, the next nap, the next walk.

This is the first time I've written in my journal since the cruise. I'm afraid I'll go crazy if I don't record some of this.

*   *   *   *

Today I went searching for the waterfall. After a week alone in the cabin with only Cinders for company I felt restless, compelled to find the waterfall despite the warning gusts of wind and darkening clouds.

I was on what seemed the right trail but getting nowhere when the storm came upon us. Suddenly it broke its waters, releasing a torrent of rain. It soaked me and everything around me: rocks, trees, Cinders, the stream. We sought shelter under a huge oak tree.

I just stood there, watching the stream swell, the drops beat a pattern into the earth, the branches bend and sway beneath the downpour, the puddles form around my feet.

To my horror, I started crying. There was no one there I had to watch out for, protect, worry about. I sobbed. I didn't know I'm so full of disappointment and grief.

The waterfall I couldn't find had come to me?

A flash of lightning was immediately followed by a rumble of thunder. Cinders pushed herself between my legs. I resisted the impulse to push her away, then felt a bolt of anger surge up through me. No more dependence! I wanted to cry out. No more little vipers who suck and suck until you shrivel up. Empty. Emptied.

"Leave me alone!" I screamed. Cinders cowered from the storm, leaned against my legs panting heavily. I scratched her head for assurance—my screams weren't aimed at her.

"Go away!" I yelled at the thunder. "I'm not your mother, I'm not your boss. Don't ask me. Leave me alone. Damn you all!" The thunder echoed my grumbling.

I've never screamed much before—never had to. Clenching my teeth and raising my voice usually did the trick. Now I yelled at the top of my lungs and no one heard me. Exhilarating. I said the most hateful things and no one was hurt. In the storm I'd met my match. No matter how much venom I released, the storm sheltered me.

But anger kept turning to tears. Screams twisted into sobs. No matter how much I poured out, more sadness welled up inside me.

Another flash of lightning lit up the woods. Cinders whimpered with me, licking my face with a concern that touched me into weeping even more. Alarmed, I ran out from beneath the tree, Cinders close behind.

That's when we were struck. I guess. An orange ball ran down one side of the oak tree. Blue and green rays shot out through its main branches. My hair rose with the current.

The tree seemed to fall in front of us, rocking the ground beneath our feet, shattering branches down upon our heads.

A charge ran through my arm and down to my feet. A numbing roar rolled around me, shutting me into a silent core. I was rooted to the ground with tremendous force. It was as if two gigantic hands gripped my ankles and tried to pull me into the ground. Suddenly the force was gone. I fell, a stabbing pain in my chest. When I came to, I couldn't move.

Later—seconds? minutes? more? I noticed Cinders lying next to me, looking stunned. When I opened my eyes, she wagged her tail. She stretched out her front paws and raised her rump as if to get up. But her rump plopped down again and instead she crawled over to me to lick my face. Her rough tongue hit some nerve that reached all the way to my toes. I could feel my legs again. My heart was pounding desperately—like someone knocking on the door of a burning house in the middle of the night.

Finally we were able to get up and check ourselves out. Neither of us seemed injured. A miracle?

All I wanted then was the safety of the cabin. The thunder was moving on, but rain steadily drenched us. Half the oak tree still stood; the other half was gashed and charred. Luckily the lightning didn't start a fire.

Enough, enough. Time to leave well enough alone. The storm listened to me. The storm struck me. I knew who was boss.

*   *   *   *

Last night I had a very strange dream. I fell to pieces. Not like the song. My legs fell off and started walking away separately. My right arm waved and sailed off in one direction, while my left arm shook a fist and marched off in another. My breasts folded up like an accordion and bounced off. It was like a modern painting. My womb grew hair like a baby animal and curled up in a hole in the ground. The pieces started fighting each other. I couldn't stop them. I shouted but they didn't hear me. I became each piece and tried to persuade the others to join me, but no one listened. I tried everything. I circled in and through each piece, but I couldn't bring them all together again.

I felt like crying when I woke up but the tears just sat in my chest like some soggy puddle.

*   *   *   *

This morning I woke to a terrified, high pitched shriek. I was groggy and staggered to the porch to switch on the light. There was Cinders soaking wet from the rain (it has rained every night for the past week). In her mouth was a small animal. "Drop it," I commanded; she obeyed. It looked like a rabbit.

I grabbed her collar and shoved her into the cabin, shutting the door. Was she bringing me this catch as a gift? Would she rip it apart and eat it?

When I crouched down, I could see it was a baby raccoon. Its little masked eyes were alert with pain and fear. Its soggy body was moving up and down, breathing with an effort. My impulse was to take it in my arms, wrap it in a blanket, and bring it into the cabin to get warm.

But it was a wild animal. What if I touched it and it bit me? I recalled all the stories about raccoons with rabies. I just stared at it for the longest time. I was so tired I couldn't do anything.

Finally in the cabin I found an old towel, a can of dog food. I edged past Cinders, panting eagerly. The baby raccoon was about the size of a young cat. It watched terrorized as I draped the towel across its body. It was shivering. When I reached across its head to place some food in front of its mouth, it screamed that desperate cry again. I dropped the food and quickly pulled back my hand.

What if its mother was looking for it? Would my smell, if I touched it, turn the mother away? I longed to scratch its little head for comfort, but I didn't want to contaminate it.

I went back inside and lay down. The window opened upon the porch. Whenever I heard a rustle, I'd poke my flashlight out and watch the baby raccoon struggling to move.

I wondered if Cinders had injured it badly? Had it been crushed by falling out of a tree? I hadn't seen any wounds, but the wetness could be blood as well as rain.

It began calling. To its mother? Not that high piercing scream, just a low call. Its soft trills sounded like a song.

The song was so sweet I imagined adopting it for a pet if its mother never came for it. My friend Nancy had a pet raccoon when she was little. She said it would wake her in the morning by lifting her eyelids with its delicate fingers.

This morning I found the baby dead. It looked like it was sleeping peacefully, but its little belly wasn't moving. Its head was resting on its front hands, its hind paws were folded over comfortably. But when I turned it over, its mouth was still open, still crying for help.

Did it die of shock? Could I have saved it? I could at least have stayed up with it. All I did was hear its song. Did it know I was listening?

I found a shovel in the shed and dug a hole next to a scraggly little pine. Before I wrapped it in the towel I touched the pad of its little black hand: so dainty, so soft, so cold. Its little baby teeth were not even grown out. How sharply could they have bitten me? After covering it with the earth and leaves I'd dug up, I placed a rock over the soft spot so Cinders wouldn't dig it up.

Back in the cabin I stared at myself in the mirror. It's so dusty I look like a ghost. I had to face myself. No more illusions I can "take care of" the rest of the world. I gave birth; I can't stop death. What remains of my caretaking is this shell, this mask that stares back at me, this object in the mirror. Worthless. Something that can't be sold or even bartered anymore.

"I can fasten on a beautiful day, as a bee fixes itself on a sunflower. It feeds me, rests me, satisfies me, as nothing else does...This has a holiness. This will go on after I'm dead."

—*Virginia Woolf*

REUNION

I've never taken this trail further than the waterfall. But Clare's game. My heart's already hammering in my ears. Here's a road—with ruts, flanked by stone walls. Surprising, out here in the woods.

What's Clare gasping at? A huge arch made of large slabs of stone. Manmade. Who? Way out here.

"The old Balm estate," she says.

I remember the stories of enormous wealth, luxurious living. "Burned down?"

"At the turn of the century."

Imagine the carriages full of elegant guests driving up the steep winding road. The ruins are fun to wander through. Only the foundation remains, a full cellar with windows, walls and doorway made of enduring stone. Beautiful stone work, craftsmanship not found anymore. But how did they do it? Out here in the woods, halfway up a mountain side.

Sunlight pouring through the walls, the windows, the doors, the roof. Trees growing inside. Life goes on. We do survive. But everything changes.

Marble pillars? No, they're wood. Fluted tree trunks? No, they're hollow. It's a wooden facade. See, one's fallen apart. On its shell initials carved.

"Too bad it isn't marble. Then they'd have to learn how to carve, like budding Michaelangelos."

"That would keep them busy."

I used to keep my kids busy with music and sports—so they wouldn't get busy with sex and drugs.

Empty swimming pool. We can only imagine reflections in the water: row of hemlocks, dancing oaks, mountain slope. What's that? Sitting in front of the pool on its own pedestal—an iron chair. A simple design. For whom? A ghost perhaps.

Our ruins do remain. Life goes on, growth all around. But the shells we leave don't grow, don't change, don't serve any useful purpose, except, sometimes, beauty.

Here's this emptiness again. Why do I feel so lonely? Hope Clare doesn't mind if I take her hand. No, she's putting her arm around me. Comforting—warm flesh among so much cold stone. The fallen log next to the empty chair makes a good place to sit.

"Sometimes it seems that everything's the same, cycling over and over, fall after fall, winter after winter, spring after spring, and summer after summer. Nothing really changes."

Two falls ago Jack was alive.

"Yes, but no fall is ever like any other fall, no summer like any other. Nothing is ever really the same."

We're both right, I guess. It doesn't feel like we are disagreeing, despite our opposing perspectives.

What's that sound—a small animal scampering away. The baby raccoon. Listening all night for her mother to come. Numbing silence. No more illusion she would return. She went begging, her mouth open, singing her last, sweet, lovely hums. Why was I so afraid to touch her? I could've worn gloves. I let her die there on that cold porch.

"Do you suppose she was abandoned by her mother?…Had her mother been killed?…Was she hungry? Was that why she ventured too close to humans?…Did she die of shock? of the cold?…There wasn't a tear on her. Cinders must've carried her gently, like when I let her bite my arm for play."

"She must have been hurting inside. She must have been already injured. Probably not much you could have done for her, hon."

"That's what I figured." This is such a familiar regret. "You know, I thought my power as a mother would sustain me forever. But the children have taken it away from me. Maybe it wasn't mine, after all."

"The children didn't take it away. We just blame our children for the emptiness of life, like they blame us."

"We women have taken too much care of things. Isn't that why my own children have turned against me?"

"Have they?"

What's the point of answering? She hasn't seen Dick's expression as he watched me struggle with the knowledge that he's totally replaced me. That self-righteous glaze. Might as well change the subject. "I saw a documentary once about grizzly bears. The farmers kept threatening to 'take care of them' for destroying their livestock. *Taking care* is so double-edged. When I think of caretakers now, I think of cemeteries."

"But what about all those hungry and homeless children, all those battered and abused children? All those children we haven't paid enough attention to?" Is she thinking of her own child? (I can't believe I never knew. I can't believe she never told me.)

My baby sister crying all night. Mama sick...gone...in the hospital, having another baby? I can't be more than three years old. Trapped in my crib. Listening to her sob, whimper, sigh.

I'm as powerless now as I was then, as I was with the baby raccoon. No use moaning—might as well move on.

Past the ruins the trail runs slantwise up the mountain. Slowly. My heart tries to burst from this cage of chest, this nest.

A huge rock slide. Grey rocks tumbling down the mountain, dramatic backdrop to the intense fall colors. These must've been the rocks used in the foundation of the mansion. Carried by the crew of skilled men—no women, I'll bet—who built this palace for the industrial czar who hired them. His discovery, this place? His vision, this house? Perhaps. Not, I'd guess, the labor of making that dream come true. Such work is never one person's only. Even when all those people surround us, we tend to forget that.

"Do you suppose the rock slide was caused by them pulling out rocks for the foundation?" The connection Clare makes is surprising.

"Or did they exploit the resources after the rocks fell?" Somehow her explanation makes more sense.

Almost as soon as I feel the impulse—of course there's no bathroom in the ruins—the tickle starts. Of all the tricks my aging body plays on me, this is the worst. As a child I felt shame. Mama didn't scold but she teased me—glad, I guess, to show me what a baby I was and not the independent cuss I pretended to be.

Giggling in the schoolyard when I was little, I had to sit down to hide it—got into trouble with the teacher for running home soon as recess was over—never told her why. Now, a mature woman, I feel humiliation. The trickle has no mercy. It will start during an important meeting, in the middle of dinner, just as production is at its peak. All it takes is a laugh, a sneeze, a surprising move. Makes me feel much older than I am.

Quick, dart behind this huge rock, squat down. It's too late. My pants, my only pants now, are soaked. After wiping myself with a tissue, I reluctantly pull the wet panties and damp slacks back on again, and join Clare.

"Accident," I murmur, in case she starts to smell something.

"Oh dear, how uncomfortable. Maybe we should go back."

"No, it's ok." I pull my coat around me. "It's so lovely here."

She's untying the scarf around her shoulders and wrapping it around my waist, "to keep the wind out." I feel like a gypsy.

Beyond the rock slide, a view of the lake. Dark blue, the water; light blue, the sky; hills dotted with evergreen patches holding their color steady while all around them leaves turn and fall, red, orange, brown, gold, yellow.

It feels so good to sit in silence, watching, listening to the leaves fall. The only sounds are wind and leaves. And the voices within our own heads: all those we want to help, who need our help, whose help we need.

"How much real power do we have?"

"Less than we think but more than we know."

"Once we're old enough to know, they're too young to care."

"Our warnings fall on deaf ears."

What about my own deaf ears, so recently fallen upon?

"Sometimes I hope what I say to people inside my own head will find a better audience than what I say out loud." It's true; Clare's sparing of spoken words.

"Don't you worry about being crazy, with all those voices inside?" I ask.

"I am crazy! What's there to worry about? I can live with it."

"Choosing which voice to listen to is what drives me crazy."

"I figure I got to listen to all of them. I can't afford to ignore a one."

"Doesn't that feel like over-stimulation—like flipping the radio dial from station to station?"

"But I don't have to obey all of them—or even any of them all of the time."

The lake, the woods, the trees, all lights and shadows playing off each other.

What's that shadow in the woods, moving? A deer? Look, Clare, she's in the clearing. So cautious. No sound but wind and leaves. She must feel safe, she's bending down to graze. That patch of green must be that groundcover I saw down there—probably planted by some gardener years ago.

A twig cracking. To our right. On a ledge below us, two hunters—in their clownish red, with guns in hand. Watching the deer too. I better move, scare them off. That one is turning, sees me. Shall I scream to warn the deer? Why's he waving so frantically?

"What's he saying?" Clare's eyesight's so much better than mine.

"He's putting down his gun, shaking his head, pointing to his chest as if he has breasts. Oh, yeah. It's a doe. He can't shoot her."

"Why not?"

"It's against the law to shoot does."

"Whew."

Clare's wiping her hand across her forehead in an exaggerated gesture of relief. The hunter is smiling.

But the deer's darting into the woods, startled by something. We've made no sound. The hunter and his friend have made no sound. Did she smell us? Her white tail's bobbing into the dark shelter of the trees. A shot rings out. The hunter's gun is resting on a rock. His friend's gun too.

A second shot. The sound of someone falling.

Standing up, too late, I yell.

Two other hunters are walking out of the woods and through the clearing. Gazing up at us. Can they see us? We shrink behind the huge boulders we've been sitting on. (Are we all stalking each other?)

"Hey!" yells our hunter pal. "She's a doe. You can't shoot her."

The two men give him the finger and walk on to look for their prey. I hope the deer's dead and not just wounded.

How disheartening. We might as well go back down the trail. I don't feel like hiking any more. There's cursing in the woods. A flurry of obscenities exchanged between the pairs of hunters. Then silence.

The carriage road winds down slowly past the ruins, bends back to join a larger road. Blocked by a red truck. On the hood of the truck, like a grotesque ornament, the body of the deer.

Shrinking again, our shared impulse seems to be to hide in the woods and watch. Why are the men in such a hurry? They tie the deer roughly to the hood. Blood's running out of her mouth. Her belly's swollen. Is she pregnant? They seem to have no satisfaction with their success. They move with quick furtive gestures like mechanical toy soldiers, ambushed. No grace in them. No hunger either, to justify the need for her meat. They come to nature armed and afraid and they leave the same way.

What's that siren sound? A forest ranger, red light on his truck flashing. With him, the other two hunters. The ranger is speaking to the ones who shot the deer. They're cursing the other two. He's putting handcuffs on them and pushing them into his truck. Seems surprisingly harsh, but maybe they're trespassing too.

"He should tie *them* on the hood." The ranger's glancing around—did he hear her whisper?

Their arrest doesn't satisfy me. Justice has been served, but the deer's still dead.

Now they've all driven off, leaving the truck and its once lovely cargo. Who will get the deer?

Edging past the truck. Suddenly I grab a rock to hurl against the windshield. How easily the pane in the old truck shatters. It's shocking—like throwing a pebble into the eye of someone wearing glasses.

"Look." Clare sounds approving. She's pointing as the sun lights up a web pattern imprinted in the splintered glass.

I touch the deer as we sneak by. I've never petted a deer before. She's still warm, but stiffening, her fur not as soft as it looks. Where's her spirit? Can it feel my touch?

Once we found a puppy that'd been struck by a car and gone into shock. We weren't sure if it was alive or dead. But when I touched it, it revived. Not this deer.

What about the baby raccoon? What if I'd dared touch her? What if I'd brought her in out of the cold?

On the trail now back past the waterfall, sun setting, Clare sees a huge spiderweb. We have to bend over to see its spectrum shining in the focused light. She touches one strand gently with her fingertip, plucking it as a harpist might sound a note. The whole web begins to vibrate, especially the center—yet nothing breaks.

Bea's Journal

Last night I had this funny dream: Someone's on trial and I'm on the jury. Except for me and another woman, all the other jurors are animals, insects and birds. I assume we're the only humans when I hear a busy whir behind me and turn to discover it comes from my own wings. Then I look down. I'm shocked to see that my arms are fuzzy. This doesn't seem to matter much.

My curiosity's drawn to the bright creature on trial, a man in Day-Glo orange.

A series of large animals are testifying against him: an elephant, who describes how he slaughtered her whole family for their ivory tusks and left their bodies rotting in the sun; a rhinoceros with thick glasses who says, "You think my horn has magical, medical, aphrodisiac qualities, but it's really useful only to me; you'd be better off chewing your own fingernails."

A whale swims in and tells her story of how the men stuck her baby with harpoons to lure her so they could kill her too.

The prosecuting attorney, a horse, speaks eloquently of the 130 species of mammals and birds now gone forever.

"Aw come off it," mutters the hunter, "now you're going to blame me for the extinction of the dinosaurs."

At this point he is attacked by several birds none of the rest of us has ever seen before. A scholarly looking turkey in the gallery shouts out their names: "the Great Auk," "the passenger pigeon," "the Carolina parakeet." The Judge, a buffalo, calls for order.

Despite the confusion of languages, it doesn't take us long to reach a verdict. The beaver and the walrus are quite impassioned on the subject, having barely escaped extinction themselves (I wonder why the defense attorney, a pig, has even allowed them on the jury. Perhaps the list of endangered species is so long, he ran out of challenges, or perhaps he too has some secret revulsion at the slaughter, being both highly intelligent and very succulent.)

"They're making things out of us people don't even need, like fur coats and necklaces," protests a sea turtle.

"They're killing us for fun, for sport," complains a goose.

Even the dreaded cobra speaks well for his own survival: "They make handbags out of my skin, but I eat the rats who eat the food that needs to feed the starving people of India. How many handbags are as helpful?" I wait for the rats to speak up, but they are silent.

No one much wants to listen to anything the cockroach has to say, but as a fellow insect, I have to sympathize. Even though I make useful products for man, he focuses mostly on my sting. Listen to all those rumors about "killer bees." Honey and wax: "Sweetness and light"? Forget it.

The poor cockroach, who looks like she's made of plastic, doesn't even bite, but she doesn't produce anything like honey or wax either. She's not the bold, invasive figure of the stereotype; she's really very timid—for good reasons. But, she confides in me during one of our breaks, "we're the real survivors. They ought to take some time to read a page from our book—'cause after they've done themselves and everybody else in, we're gonna still be here."

"Guilty" is an easy verdict for us to reach but we contest the sentence hotly. The humanitarians, of course, plead that we "save the hunters," showing them compassion they haven't shown us. "Save the hunters from themselves" is their refrain. None of these defenders, I note, are vegetarians. The human member of the jury, to our surprise, doesn't take this position. She suggests a "fitting punishment" would be to hang the hunter by a thread until it breaks, so he will know what it feels like to become extinct.

Oh my god, I realized when I woke up, this dream isn't about animal rights, it's about my own extinction. I know nothing has really changed—I'm still who I am—but on some other level, I feel like an endangered species. It's terrifying.

"I could not bear the Bees should come…
They're here, though; not a creature failed…—
In gentle deference to me—
The Queen of Calvary."
—Emily Dickinson

TRIALOGUE

▼

"Women and power" sounds much like an oxymoron. Certainly a contradiction. Every day women are raped, shot, enslaved, abused, dismissed, humiliated, mocked. Nowhere around the globe do I know of any entire nation where women as a group have the upper hand, although there are stories of matriarchal cultures hidden away in remote communities.

Yet we all know powerful women, in history or in our own lives: Catherine the Great or Elizabeth the First, Mary Magdalene or Hildegarde of Bingham; our mothers, whether their power was positive or negative; women we admire The women I admire most are the ones who had the courage to speak truth to power or to subvert the power of tyranny or evil, women like Rosa Parks, Elizabeth Gurley Flynn, Rosa Luxemburg, and Wangari Maathai. Or women whose power is demonstrated by their love for others, not just their own people, their passion for justice. Without such women, the rest of us would not have the right to vote, to own property, to have custody of our own children, to resist marital rape, to be employed rather than be owned or exploited, to leave abusive husbands, to inherit, to be educated, to run for office.

When we speak of power in women, we mean three different kinds of power in three different contexts: maternal power, patriarchal power, and collective power. Many, certainly not all, women are powerful as mothers or grandmothers, in charge of their own homes and families, the private realms. As midwives and healers, women in this realm are the gatekeepers over the mysteries of life and death, powerful enough in medieval times to be burned at the stake. In most cultures, not just the mother-blaming western psychological realm, mothers are powerful in the lives of their children, although rarely powerful enough to protect them from outside threats: wars, poverty, or disasters both natural and manmade.

Some people like to ally this maternal power with their fantasy of matriarchal power, but despite some wonderful fictional and anthropological speculations about such an archy, we have little idea what a world actually structured by women free of patriarchal socialization, and run by women, would feel and look like. We can only hope it would be better. The closest actual archetype we have of such a world is the Iroquois Confederacy, whereby male leaders are chosen and guided by a counsel of older women. Although their system became a model for our United States constitution, somehow the council of wise elders got lost along the way. (Thank goddess we have AARP.)

Some women are powerful by way of a powerful man, their fathers, their husbands, their brothers, or their mentors; they survive in the world of work and politics by playing by the patriarchal rules, and usually by being more competent, more productive, and more conscientious than their male peers. These "exceptional women" may never completely smash through the glass ceiling or be invited to join the men's club but they know how to profit from the old boy networks and to set up a few parallel networks of their own.

Martha Stewart is an interesting example of such a powerful woman in that she applied patriarchal rules of success to the maternal realm of the domestic arts. She made and lost her fortune by those same rules, and paid the price of sticking out like a sore, albeit green, thumb in the world of corporate wheeling and dealing. The fact that she was sent to jail over what was an essentially victimless crime, cheating and lying about one transaction, while men who defrauded their companies of millions of dollars, impoverishing their own tens of thousands of employees, still move from one mansion to another, suggests that gender still holds its biases even for successful, powerful women.

Most of us women, however powerful we may be in our own families, churches, schools or workplaces, are not exceptional in that sense. Neither are most men. The only way we can experience real power is collectively. Allied with maternal power, collective power can be quite daunting. Witness the grandmothers of Argentina in search of their disappeared family members or the mothers in Russia who literally pulled their sons out of the military to keep them from fighting in an unpopular war. Collectively these courageous women won out over the powers that be.

Contemporary women are wary of a concept of power which has been so tainted by patriarchy that it can mean only "power *over* others." Most women instinctively know, from observation and from experience, that power *over* others solidifies a person so much that he begins to harden, like a concrete statue. Eventually he feels so heavy he's in danger of tripping and, if he falls, crushing himself. He carries the burden of dominance in his own petrified self. Despite its rewards in terms of status, money, control and influence, such power is not appealing enough that most sane and healthy people rush to embrace it. With their double burden of jobs and families, sometimes triple burden with the care of elders, women's backs are already loaded: as Zora Neale Hurston reminded us, we're "the mules of the world,"

Some feminist theorists have claimed their power within the Frierean notion of a temporary imbalance of power, such as parent with child, teacher with student, therapist with client, which comes to equilibrium through the nurturing or healing relationship between them: the child growing up to care for the parent; the mentee becoming a colleague of the mentor; the client being the equal of the therapist, perhaps by eventually becoming a therapist. In the dynamic field of relationships, this model recognizes that power shifts from person to person as roles change, as resources are made mutual. Power is not institutionalized. Leadership is shared. Authority is communal in nature. We take responsibility for each other, we learn from each other, and we heal each other despite our established roles.

Others are more comfortable with the concept of *agency*, that personal power which can lift us out of a state of feeling powerless. Agency is the capacity to own and take responsibility for one's own life, to self-actualize, to self-create—as well as the ability to get things done. Certainly in most contexts women are every bit as capable as men of getting things done. In many situations they are the ones who actually do the work required to keep a group or an institution alive and growing. I've often thought that if we could bloodlessly lop off the heads of our institutions, those bodies would function a lot more efficiently and humanely. All that vertical energy which goes toward placating, appeasing, justifying oneself to the bosses could go toward horizontal collegiality or service to those for whom the institution was designed.

Which is not to say we don't need leaders, people whose vision, confidence, enthusiasm, and courage help us move collectively around obstacles and over pitfalls, people whose own endurance, devotion to a cause, concern for the mission or generosity toward the people involved inspires others to emulate their actions. But these are usually not the kind of people who are comfortable in set roles of command and control, within hierarchical organizations, with the kind of stasis that institutional bureaucracies require. The best leaders are comfortable in dynamic, democratic, collaborative, and creative movements, whether for the good of a certain group or for the good of a whole society.

When it comes to power, Bea is a powerful woman. She has more than her share of agency. She was, at least at the beginning of her career, a creative, effective leader. She is powerful both in the private realm, as a mother, and in the public realm, as a innovator and entrepreneur. But, well schooled in the disciplines of western individualism, she doesn't have a clue about collective power, about how to share power, or what to do with power beyond personal achievement and financial success.

Ultimately, the question of power depends on what it is used for. Power itself is neutral, a kind of dynamic energy which can be used for good or for ill. Bea's sense of self was invested in the capitalistic notion that individual accomplishment represents the pinnacle of power. When it became burdensome, she tried to hand it over—but the point of personal satiety or fulfillment is the very cusp where collective power can be used for a greater good, to address imbalances of wealth or privilege, to create new initiatives for healing the world, to share one's accumulated resources with others, beyond the personal realm where one is still tempted to use power to control and manipulate others. Bea retired just when she could have made a meaningful difference in her world. Instead of pushing her limits at the height of her power, she gave up—retreated. But perhaps that's the only way she could redeem herself.

PART THREE:
THE HIVE

This we know:
All things are connected
Like the blood
Which unites one family...

Whatever befalls the earth,
Befalls the sons and daughters of the earth.
Man did not weave the web of life;
He is merely a strand in it.
Whatever he does to the web,
He does to himself.

—Ted Perry, inspired by Chief Seattle

DICK

Eldest child of Bea and Jack, number one son, a lawyer, executive of Harmony Enterprises, brother of Bruce, Cory and John, husband of Jeanne, father of Todd, Angela and Cassie, grandson of Mildred.

C'mon, old man, he thought, gripping the steering wheel. *It says "yield," not "nap."*

Dick was in control of his black BMW and raring to go. But here he was stuck behind a lollygaging white-haired tourist-type who didn't seem to care where he was going or how fast he got there. Dick glanced at himself in the rear view mirror, admiring his handsome, square features. The gray at his temples was distinguished yet inconspicuous next to his blondish waves, and his green eyes sparkled.

Boy, ever since she announced her retirement, he thought, bouncing in the plush seat, *I feel so revved up. I've got new ideas, I've got tons of energy. It's about time. She's done a great job, been a great model, but it's time for new blood.*

The driver in front of him moved forward, then hesitated as the traffic streamed by. *Yeah, go on, inch out,* Dick coached. *It's not going to kill you. The snail's pace is what'll kill you. Move!*

The driver did not move as directed. Dick groaned and switched on the radio. It was the weather report. Boring. He switched it off and continued to obsess about where he was going.

I know we could make a fortune if we could just hit the higher education market, he thought. *But that's going to take some aggressive salesmanship as well as a ton of vision. She just doesn't move fast enough anymore. If she'd grabbed that university contract when I told her to, we...but she kept saying we weren't ready yet. We lost it. Fuck it, I was ready.*

Finally the flow of traffic stopped and the driver ahead of him cautiously moved out. Fortunately he was going in the opposite direction. The tires squealed as Dick sped out and headed for the expressway.

Used to be she'd move fast, he thought as he drove up the ramp, *she'd head straight for the target, and she got ahead of just about everybody. Now she meanders in one direction, wanders around in circles, gets nowhere fast. More like she acted when we were little kids—always distracted. Even as late as my high school graduation, her focus was fuzzy. There we were tossing our caps in the air, like they do at Annapolis: my moment of glory, tops in my class, I turn to see her proud face and she isn't even looking at me. She's straightening John's tie and brushing the hair out of his eyes. Once in my life I graduate; fifty times a day he's got hair in his eyes. Talk about concentration. Now her head's going soft like that again.*

Dick pulled into the fast lane and began to zip past other cars while he kept an eye out for a patrol car. He could feel the tension in his arms and chest as he held the big car steady on the road, a tension which was as familiar to him as the air he breathed.

That's just aging, I guess, he told himself. *Check out how flaky Gram has become. That's why I need to take over now—before I get flabby myself.* He looked down at the slight paunch below the rim of the steering wheel, resolving to play golf more regularly. Thinking about inheriting his mother's position as CEO of the company charged him up. *I've got the drive, I've got the thrust, I've got the smarts, and I've got the connections this company needs.*

Ahead he saw flashing red lights and quickly pulled over into the slow lane, behind a pickup truck. Some unlucky bozo was handing his driver's license out the window to a police officer. Chances were, this was the only uniform in the area, so as soon as the red lights disappeared in the rear view mirror, he sped up again.

With Mom no longer pulling strings, bouncing us up and down like a bunch of puppets, he thought, *I'll really be able to push us forward. I gotta give her credit though; she recognizes when the show is over, when it's time for the new generation to take charge. And she's really done an excellent job.* He felt almost choked up when he thought of all his mother had accomplished and prayed he could be both as successful and worthy of her rare praise.

Suddenly the cars ahead of him slowed to a crawl. *I can't believe this traffic,* he groaned. The whole world must be trying to get an early start this morning. He glanced at his watch. *I better get a phone in this car,* he decided.

He tried to switch lanes but nobody would let his big car in front of them. *I just hope everyone else doesn't oppose everything I want to do,* he thought. *Clare and Pearl might get in the way. Chances are they'll follow Mom's lead; they always have. They've done their time. I don't want to be the one to have to put them out to pasture, but I know I can show them some real profits, make them proud they backed the right man for the job.*

Trapped in the car, Dick continued to obsess. *Bruce will be no problem. He's too spineless to object to anything I do, and most of the time he knows I'm right. Corey and John could care less about the business—as long as they get their dividend checks. I really do have everyone's best interests at heart. I'm worth their investment.*

Suddenly a young woman petting a dog next to her in the front seat hesitated before she could close the gap and decisively he edged his car into the flow. It was only a trickle but better than the other lane, which had dried up completely.

Much more of Mom's backing up and the business will be heading for financial disaster, he thought. *We're gonna need someone with my will and foresight to pull us through. I just hope they have the sense to give me more control. I'm tired of them nodding sweetly at my suggestions, then ignoring them completely. I'm a grown man, for chrissake. It's time she acknowledged how much she depends on me. My legal expertise has pulled us through many a tight spot.*

Finally he passed an accident, nothing more than a fender bender but enough to clog the morning rush, and the traffic picked up again.

Soon enough they'll all be proud of me, he thought, straightening his Armani tie in the mirror. *Jeanne'll get so turned on, she'll want me to fuck her all the time. The kids will boast about me to all their friends. Even Gram will admit I didn't turn out so bad. Mom will finally appreciate me. I'll move this family into the twenty-first century and make us all rich in the process.*

He grinned as he exited the expressway and headed for work. *I'm not my mother's son for nothing.*

*   *   *   *

No matter what I do, how powerful I become, she still turns away. She pulls the blanket up over that iceberg of a shoulder and goes to sleep. I thought she found powerful men attractive. Maybe I can just press up against her. Jesus, now she's wincing away. How subtle.

She owes it to me. For all I do for her. Women get the soft life, they get to be like children: dependent, easy, emotional. They're allowed to avoid war, violence, competition, hard work. Serves 'em right when men show them that side of life once in a while.

No, I'm not that kind of a guy. All I want is to be part of that softness once in awhile, sink myself into it and rest a bit. This energy inside just can't stop. If I could push it inside her for a while, it could rest. It's like putting my car in the garage—where it's safe, resting until its next venture out.

Gotta get those tires checked. All I need at the moment is a flat. But I barely have time to get the tank filled and the oil checked these days. It's always such a hassle crawling around with that gauge, but the attendants won't help anymore. Why do something for nothing?

We need to revive the concept of service.

Jeanne's always shoving me out. I'm too much for her: too big, too eager, too much passion, too much. I ought to just shove it in her anyway, like some men do with their wives. What kind of wimp am I? She'll end up enjoying it. They always do. No, no, no, then yes, yes, oh yes.

Yes, she says, yes. She slides into my office and presses up against me. She's got to have me now. Harriet, my secretary, enters just as she's coming down on me. She joins us. She's hot. I have them both. They groan with pleasure as I enter them. One after the other and then I start all over again. They love it.

Shit, she's gone to the bathroom. She won't come out for an age. She's so tense all the time. This would probably help. I won't shove it in. I'll just ease it in when she falls asleep. Like I'm doing with this pillow. Oh yeah, oh yeah. But flesh would be so much warmer. Oh, ohhhh. Yeah.

I want her to love it, but she doesn't. She used to pretend she did, but now she's so secure, she doesn't even bother.

Here she comes. Now I don't need her. Let her settle for a pillow.

Once, right while I was watching, John gave Mom a long intense kiss right on the lips. He was about four, I guess. I was amazed she let him get away with it. You could've knocked me over with a pillow. And when he pulled away, with a huge grin on his face, she just laughed. Whenever I hugged her, she stiffened. Maybe that's why he's such a queer.

What the hell. I'm going back to someone who does enjoy it. Who can't get enough of me. "She's got that magic touch." I'll call her into the office as soon as I get to work tomorrow.

Honey pie, open those friendly, welcoming arms. Here I come.

$$* \qquad * \qquad * \qquad *$$

One advantage of driving to work late is less traffic. I can just whiz along.

Better call Carmichel about this promotion idea…"Tim? Chance here. Let me run this by you—for the new brochure: "New ideas are built on the ruins of the old [period] People with vision make them work [period] [Bullet] Better quality [dash, bullet] improved customer service [dash] provide greater security [period] Satisfied customers are our best security [period]" Like it? Ok, then, let's go with it."

I hope this new line will persuade Kramer to go with us. We've got to emphasize service now there's more competition. Mom's high-handed, take-it-or-leave-it approach just won't cut it anymore.

Watch it, lady. Whoever taught you how to drive?

It took all my pull and quite a bit of my money to get Union Suburban to accept John. Just because he doesn't have any medical insurance? What'd they care, long as someone pays? I guess they have their classy reputation to uphold.

Clare doesn't realize what a favor's she done me by kidnapping Gram. Now Mom can decide what to do with her. Obviously she's off her rocker, but I don't want to be the one to commit her. I'm tired of being the fall guy around here. You try to do what's best for everyone and all they do is hassle you. As if I didn't have enough on my mind: the deal with Kramer, the safety inspection.

Was John grateful? Of course not. All he wanted was to see Bea. To wait for Corey. To stay home. I explained to him there was no one here to care for him. I didn't dare explain how hysterical Jeanne got when she found out he's so sick. She's terrified of germs—but can you catch pneumonia from somebody else? Anyway he was too weak to argue. So off he went in style, ambulance and all. Nothing but the best for my little brother.

No one can say I'm not generous with my family—despite their crazy life-styles. And if this deal goes through, I'll be able to be even more lavish. Just my luck to have this surprise safety inspection. Did Pearl leak something out? According to Opal, she was snooping around. Naw—what proof does she have? At least we've gotten notice, so we can set things right before they get here. But if we don't pass, the contract with Kramer will be very shaky.

If Clare and Mom want to take care of Gram, the more power to them. At least it's out of my hands. Haven't I got enough on my mind? I don't think any of them realize how much I do for everyone. Makes me appreciate Mom more—all she had to do to keep things going.

I wonder if John's on drugs. He looks awful. Course he's been fruity looking since day one—but now he's lost maybe twenty pounds since the party, his hair looks funny, and his face looks like he's just been released from a concentration camp.

We didn't ask any questions. We just put him up in the guestroom. Since he was looking for Mom, I was going to lend him a car to drive up there in the morning. But that night Jeanne overheard him telling Corey on the phone what was wrong with him. She panicked. I'd like to know what's so frightening about pneumonia—but she's compulsive about germs in the house.

She's already suspicious about why I'm late at the office so much. Starting to call there at night. How many times can I let the answering machine cover for me—or chat with her right in the midst of a good fuck? So I knew John had to go, soon. I'm not about to stay home and take care of him myself, and I sure can't count on her to do it.

Oh shit, what's wrong with my focus? I need to concentrate on this safety inspection—make sure there aren't any loose ends. It's not so much the fine that bothers me if we're caught—but I sure don't need that slur on our reputation. We're known as a family business: honest, fair, generous to our employees...

Luckily he started coughing to beat the band. The doctor I called agreed the hospital would be the best place for him.

Then John blew it by telling them at the hospital he doesn't have insurance. Fool. What a time to announce his deficiencies. That's why I had to pull all those strings. This little hospital stay is going to put me out at least a grand. But it's worth it to get Jeanne off my back for awhile.

*   *   *   *

What a nightmare. They'd vandalized my car. Wires dangling where the stereo had been. Oil pouring out. Gas tank empty. They'd stolen everything. All the insides exposed, hanging out. They'd been caught in the act, but their business mostly was done. Shit, I'm panting now as if it were true. A relief to be awake.

No, not a relief. Here's yesterday's fiasco. What happened? What'd they do to me? It was like I was possessed.

...*She makes me go to this school. They make me wear this uniform and march to class. We have to get up at dawn. We have to pass inspection. We have to obey orders. We have to be good at sports. We can't smoke. We can't drink. We can't get bad grades. We can't mess with girls. I want to go home...*

It wasn't fair. Mom kicked me out and let him stay. He got to be the baby and he got to stay home too. She made me go and she didn't make him go. Said she wasn't sure it was such a good idea after all. So I get to be the guinea pig. When I don't turn out so good, everything changes. She kept him home so she could pamper him. Course that's why he's such a wimp now. I got used to it. Made me more of a man.

But I was only thirteen, for chrissake. I didn't want to go. I had my friends at home I wanted to stay with. They made me go. Dad backed her up. Said it would have done him a world of good to go to prep school when he was my age. Guess he was right. It has made all the difference. Look where I am now compared to where John is.

Prep school might have been ok, but I didn't want to have to live there. It could have been a reform school; most of us felt like rejects. Why didn't they want us at home? What had we done wrong? What were they afraid we'd do wrong? Some of the big guys were real mean. Some of the little guys were real fairies. But we all got something out of it in the long run. Toughened us up. No fairies now.

I was her "little man." As soon as the babies came along, I was on my own. And not just on my own: I was supposed to help take care of them. I was just a kid myself, but I took care of them, and I did a hell of a good job. Not sure she could've managed it all without me. Dad was never home except on weekends— then we all had to make things easier for him.

If it hadn't been for the other kids, if it hadn't been for the business, if it hadn't been for Dad—if it hadn't been for all that, things might have turned out different. I might not feel so ripped off. I might be more relaxed. I might be more fun. I might not turn people off. It's her fault. She's to blame.

But they'd rather blame me. If I hadn't had it so rough I might not be running the business for them and taking care of them after they keep fucking up their lives. Can't you just see a wimp like John trying to do the job I'm doing? But no, they can't see that, they'd rather jump all over me. I didn't ask for this. Little man is ok, but big man's a big problem.

Sure she prefers John—he's so wimpy and soft and pliable, no threat to her. I'm too much of a man for her. That's what she gets for sending me away. And that lump in the bed is what she gets for keeping him at home.

BRUCE

Second son of Bea and Jack, a salesman for Harmony Enterprises, younger brother of Dick, older brother of Corey and John, husband of Barbara, father of Lisa and Larry, a Vietnam Veteran, grandson of Mildred.

Bruce sat in the middle of the kitchen, a rock in a stream, while Barbara his wife flowed around him, preparing the evening meal. His long, lean body folded in upon itself as he slumped over the kitchen table, his head resting on his hand. He felt exhausted and looked older than his limp ponytail of dark hair and trim dark beard might suggest. Darkness circled his eyes as they followed her around the room.

She knows I want a glass of milk, he thought. *She's queen of the refrigerator. I don't even have to ask.* She opens the door, removes the carton, pours a glass full.

Now she'll walk slowly up to me and pour it over my head, he told himself. *Just watch. Feel the cold shock. You didn't expect it. You didn't believe me. Like lava it moves slowly through my hair, sticking to each strand. The liquid rolls down my fore-head into my eyebrows, splashes down my cheeks. "Tears of milk"—like a good country song.*

Lost in his daydream, his focus shifted. Following the flow of milk, Mom's voice, her words snapping, "You want spilt milk? Have a whole glass!"

Surprised, he sees a glass being handed to him, hears Barbara's voice, her words, "Hard day, honey?"

No, he didn't have a hard day, but still it had been hard. He'd goofed up again, mixed up one order with another, forgot to call a customer back. Still the klutz, still knocking over glasses full, he thought of himself. Still needing this daily dose of pity. And someone there to mop it up when it sloshes over. He nod-ded, took the glass from her and gulped it down, gasping at its coldness, slightly repulsed by how thickly it coated his throat.

Later she said she was sorry, he recalled. *But I just shrugged. I didn't forgive her. That was the only power I had over her. It was the only time she ever apologized to me.*

He sat back, folded his arms into the hollow of his chest and watched Barbara pulling leftovers from the icebox. *No way she's giving up control. No way. That woman's born to rule. The day she stops pulling all the strings is the day she dies. Whatever she's trying to prove, she'll never stop controlling us.*

Although he hadn't asked, Barbara reported to him where the kids were this afternoon. One was at basketball practice; the other was sleeping over with a friend. He didn't really care. They were more her children than his. He could feel her irritation at his indifference, but of course she'd never come out and ask him why he was such a lousy father. She'd suffer in silence.

They complain they're powerless, but they totally control our lives, he thought. *Even the mild ones like Barbara who sits small and talks small and practically apologizes for entering the room. She acts like she's waiting for someone to slap her back against the wall. She knows I'll never do that to her. That's why she married me. I married her thinking she would never control me. Ha. She's subservient where Mom's domineering, uncertain where Mom's arrogant, retiring as Mom will never be, retirement or not.*

But even the meek ones control this earth, he told himself as he unwound himself to stand up and stare out of the window at the neighbor's garage. *They manipulate us. They make us feel guilty. They take over space and fill it with their feelings. They use the kids to get to us.*

Barbara asked him whether he wanted hamburgers or meatloaf for dinner. He shrugged. She'd probably already decided and if he choose the wrong thing, she'd sigh and turn away from him until he switched to the right choice. *When she really wants something,* he thought, *her will is iron—forged by her father's temper. Of course she never wants anything for herself—no, no, never. If she did, we could at least fight it out. Or figure it out. No, it's always for my good, for the kid's good, for the neighbor's good, for the world's good.*

Damn all this goodness, he thought as he exited the kitchen deliberately without asking about her pitiful day. *Doesn't she ever want to scream out? Doesn't she ever just want to belt us the way her father belted them? Doesn't she ever want to wallow in worldly pleasures instead of working her fingers to the bone for the rest of us?*

In the living room he sank into his favorite chair and took up the newspaper Barbara had put there for him. But he didn't read it.

She wants me to give a speech at her party, he recalled. *She can't accept the fact that she has a stammering idiot for a son. Like the time the teacher kept me after school because I couldn't give a speech about the family's vacation. What business was it of hers what we did? Hell, it took me a week just to squeeze out the word "summer." She didn't care how hard it was. She didn't care how much the other kids snickered, how often she had to chide them to "keep quiet and stop making fun of him." And Mom didn't care either. I begged her to talk to the teacher. I begged her to let me change schools. But teachers were her gods; she wasn't going to interfere. She said it would be good for me. It was torture. The harder you try to speak right, the worse it gets. I finally sputtered out a few words. The old bat took pity. I got to go home on time.*

He tossed down the newspaper and went over to the liquor cabinet. *Oh, what the hell?* he thought, pouring himself a gin and tonic. *All I need is to keep free of them. Let them control the world. Let the Beas and Dicks fight it out. Let the Barbaras win by losing. I won't let it touch me. I'll go someplace where all their judgments about success and failure, wealth and status, getting ahead or falling behind mean nothing. Nothing.*

After a few sips, he began to feel better, more reconciled with himself. He sat down again and pushed the recliner back so his feet were higher than his head. Nowhere to go, nothing to do.

I may not be the most aggressive person in the world, he told himself. *I may not be the brightest. I may not have much talent—but I know something they don't— damned if I'm going to tell them.* He took another gulp of his drink, savoring his secret.

*   *   *   *

This daring young man is a flying machine. I soar in my metal shell high above the nagging earth. I swoop and dive with sheer abandon.

Up here I speak my own language and I speak it fluently. It's a grammar of twists and turns, flips and rolls. My whole self somersaults and cartwheels, and everything is changed. The world seen upside down or inside out will never be the same.

No one here but clouds. They shift and dissolve into form after form. They melt away as I penetrate them. No one here to urge me on or warn me to slow down or worry about my performance or wait for me to swell the bank account or dish out allowances. No yawling babies, sniffling kids, sullen teenagers to call me Dad while they whine, complain, talk back. No meddling women, busybodies, gossips, bosses. No know-it-alls, smart alecks, eggheads. Nobody but me and my gleaming armor.

High above the ground, I look down with scorn at all those creeping, crawling creatures. I even feel a little sorry for them as they wear their ruts even deeper. There I too have been, trapped in those petty routines. But not now, not here, never again.

I watch them scurry from one greasy worry spot to another, anxious in between like rabbits in an open field. I see how they zigzag between crises they help create. They scramble from one to another although clear paths lie in between. They dig holes for dolts like me to fall into so they can rescue us.

They weave traps out of responsibility and lure us with sweetness and light. They catch us in their double binds like a preying/praying mantis and crush us with guilt. They indulge so they can disapprove. They drudge so they can begrudge. They need our helplessness so they can be so helpful.

I drift in this blissful silence. I sail through this peaceful blue. I glide over farms and fields, along the river's edge, over the mountain peaks. With grace and dash this plane and I are one. At the slightest impulse from my mind, this machine body turns, dips, glides and flips.

Sometimes the whole world opens up and expands. In this space nothing seems so bad. Even our grungy, daily living becomes magical. I can see the generosity behind Barbara's devotion to duty. I can sense the need for respect behind Dick's taking charge. I can feel my own sweet side, for a moment.

Then I dip behind a cloud and come out a dragon.

To think the air force wouldn't accept me, wouldn't let me fly. Not bright enough, they implied. Me with my eagle eye, my sixth sense, my nose for the prey, my pinpoint focus.

Like the falcon I surge up and plummet down at unbelievable speed. I seize my supper, squirming and screaming, in my talons, tighten my death grip. Then I spread my powerful wings and shoot for the heights…where no one can touch me.

*   *   *   *

Between her cracking up and me crashing, it's real hard to keep my focus clear. Why's she making all these cracks about "crack"?

"I'll just open the window a crack," she'll announce, then give me a funny look.

"Step on a crack, break your mother's back," she'll chant.

It's like she's dropping hints. It's like she knows. It started that night she watched "48 Hours on Crack Street," that god-awful special on cocaine. At first I thought it was her obsession with new words; she always runs them into the ground. But this is too much.

It's hard to tell with these older women. They act like they know something, but when you question them, they act like they don't know. Is it all smoke and no fire? Or is she trying to needle me (ha ha) into fessing up?

It gives me the creeps. Maybe Jeanne is right; maybe she's ripe for the nursing home. I don't really think she's a candidate for the funny farm though. She may just have a touch of senile dementia.

Just this morning she asked, that stupid grin on her face, if she could crack open a couple of eggs for me.

"Sounds like you're cracking up," I joked back.

Hell, I can't send my own grandmother away. She's the one who had time to let me sit on her lap. She used to read me stories. Ferdinand the Bull who refused to fight. (Sure wish I had listened more carefully to that tale.) She used to let me tell her stories. She paid no mind to my stutter. She was my only friend. Later when she started studying literature, she'd read me poems.

How'd that one go, the one I loved? Shit, I lost it. Up there when I'm flying, the way clouds dissolve and merge and disappear seems wonderful. Down here, it feels like I keep missing something, keep losing myself.

How could she know? Has she been snooping around? Would she recognize what it was if she found some? I better be more careful. It was always hard for me to keep secrets from her.

What would Mom say if we deported Gram? What right does she have to say anything? Hasn't she copped out on her responsibilities?

Were things always this screwed up? Did everything fall apart when Dad died? Nobody trusts anybody anymore. Didn't we look out for each other when we were kids? Now it's every man for himself. Survival of the fittest. Most families don't work. It's not just ours. We just looked like we had it made. But so much of that was phoniness.

Maybe families just can't work. The people don't choose to be together. Except husband and wife. And chances are, once the glow wears off, they're not so sure.

Whenever I come crashing back into my life like this, I have real doubts about my marriage. Who is this stranger I'm tied to?

What to do about Gram? She better ease up on these cracks or I'm gonna start climbing the walls.

Maybe I'll call Dick. See what he thinks. He's got more options up his sleeves than I do. He's not afraid to step on a few toes.

After all, Gram, as they say, you can't make an omelet without breaking a few eggs.

*   *   *   *

Must be John's friend (lover)...standing next to Corey. Dark. Could be Puerto Rican, or part Black. Odd that he's named "Scott." I want to go up to him after the funeral. I want to shake his hand, show him I'm not afraid to touch him.

Looks a little like my buddy Al. Before the V.C. got to him.

The minister's reading. From the Gospel of John. "Lord, if you had been here, my brother would have been saved."

Jesus says, I imagine, "Then maybe now I can be saved. Isn't one sacrifice enough? Didn't John die that I may live?"

No more "Jesus saves." Only "Jesus is saved"? From what? Is there anything worse than death?

This is not the Gospel of John. This is the Gospel according to Bruce. According to Bruise. The Old Bruiser. Me?

What would the Gospel According to Our John be like? "Love the stranger who is your brother. Love your brother who is a stranger." Did John love me? Did I love John?

This dark stranger is attractive.

Now I remember that poem. See, nothing is ever really lost. "Better strangle the helpless infant than nurse unfulfilled desires." Is that it? But what about: nurse unfulfilled desires and end up strangling the wailing child? "He who desires and acts not breeds pestilence."

"Yes, but better the road less traveled than taking the high road to nowhere."

"Lord," said Peter, "why can't I follow you now? I will lay down my life for you." Jesus answered, "Will you lay down your life for me? Truly, truly I say to you, the cock will not crow, till you have denied me three times."

And I say unto you, oh lord, my cock has not crowed thrice in a hell of a long time. At first it crowed to beat the band, but now the higher I get, the less it needs to rise.

"If the world hates you, know that it has hated me before it hated you."

That puts gays in a hell of a good position to join Jesus in heaven. John must be there now. Shit, is this guy implying Jesus himself had homosexual tendencies? Where'd they find this minister?

"When Jesus saw his mother and the disciple whom he loved standing near, he said to his mother, 'Woman, behold your son.' Then he said to the disciple, 'Behold, your mother.' And from that hour the disciple took her to his own home."

Does this mean Scott will be taken into the family fold? The Pieta all over again. Another opportunity for me to love the stranger who is my brother. Apparently Dick got his licks in. Dick a fag? That's a hot one. But St. John doesn't lie.

John doesn't lie? Whatta farce. He kept his whole life a secret from us. Hard to imagine our little Johnny a flaming Queen.

Are secrets lies? If so, I'm no longer a liar. Oh Lordy, my secret's out, out of the closet, out of the clothes hamper, out of my control. Have mercy. Who am I praying to?

"This is my beloved son in whom I am well pleased."

Son, behold thy mother. Mother, behold thy son. Mother, are you well pleased in me? You were well pleased with John. He was your beloved one. Fruity as the day is long, but your fave anyway.

Do we always lose the ones we love?

"Love is a rose and you better not pick it. Only grows when it's on the vine."

The hand that rocks the cradle nourishes the unfulfilled desire. The hand that rocks the cradle pours the milk. The hand that rocks the cradle strangles the stranger. Better not empty the desire or you will fill the womb and create the child you want to kill.

What if I'd been an only child? Would I have come stammering into this world? Would I have been a wimp at the age of three, a coward at seven, a lump at sixteen, target practice at twenty-one and an addict at twenty-five?

"This is my commandment, that you love one another as I have loved you. Greater love has no man than this, that he lay down his life for his friends."

Oh, John, why didn't I at least hug you before you died? I am not in myself well pleased.

Come out of the darkness of that damn coffin, Orpheus. Play for us.

No sound but the minister's syrupy tones.

Will we ever get to the music?

"...Mortal, my friend must be...
Barbs has it, like a Bee!
Ah, curious friend!
Thou puzzlest me!"
—Emily Dickinson

CLARE

Manager for Harmony Enterprises, Bea's aide, Mildred's friend, mother of Curtis.

This event Clare was reluctantly in charge of, but not able to control. As the guests steamed in, greeting Bea, the guest of honor, Clare prayed nothing would go wrong.

Clare herself was dressed to kill, overdressed for her own comfort with auburn hair pulled up, jewelry, long silk skirt, and higher heels than felt safe. With her sturdy figure and plain face, she knew she looked better in more tailored outfits, but Bea would have been offended if she didn't go all out. Being dolled up like this felt to Clare like a straitjacket.

Yep, she thought, watching Bea shine. You're in your glory now—Queen Bea, for real.

If you ask me, Clare said to herself from background safety, *retiring at 55 is nuts.* But nothing she said could stop Bea. She was willful as ever.

Well, you ain't retired yet, she thought, enjoying how Bea obviously dazzled everybody. Still spreading the charm around, still trying to make up for all that sharpness.

She noted that John had even let Bea get his beard trimmed. Corey must be hiding her unshaved legs under that long gown. Did Bea notice how radiant Corey looked?

What made Bea so keen on appearance anyway? Half the folks, Clare thought, *never notice what anyone wears; most the others only check to make sure they're look-ing better. Only mothers care enough to fuss—makes 'em look bad if their kids look bad.*

She wondered what John and Corey were giggling about? Had they planned something extra for tonight? They sure did speak Bea's praises. Why didn't she just relax with them? So what if they also played her edges—look how the older ones stiffen by Bea's side, their wives and children hovering in the background, intimidated. Bea shouldn't forget this other side, the one she'd tucked away in mothballs when the business started to boom, the one Corey and John risk being.

One of these days, Clare was going to say these things to Bea's face. Maybe after she retired.

How you mock weakness, she said silently to Bea, *your own teasing, how you do to us what hurt you. How people show you only their strengths, or pretend. How by pulling the best out of us, you expect too much. Haven't I seen your disappointment? Haven't I heard your bitterness?*

If someone suffered from bad luck or social prejudice, Bea was compassionate enough. But God help them if they lacked character or will power.

How gracefully Bea had taken her in when Clare showed up at her door looking for work. Could Bea tell how desperate she was? Or was she just as desperate for help? She didn't judge Clare's lack of expertise. She didn't mind training her. Clare's "managerial apprenticeship." Changed her life.

When Bea believes in someone, Clare thought, *she'll move heaven and earth to help them up. She has that gift to see the possibility. And she catches us all up in her enthusiasm, she seems to have no end of energy, nothing keeps her down for long—and she really is so magnetic.*

Clare was hurt they hadn't asked her to testify tonight. She knew more about the business than anyone, more than Pearl, more than Jack. She'd been a good ear for Bea's doubts, for hard times. Why was Bea leaving her out now? Because Clare was a little rough around the edges still?

Clare'd warned Corey and John that tributes were expected, and when—even though she hated being Bea's nag.

Bea glided through the crowd with the poise of a Queen, but Clare could see that her crusty side was out. Calling her "Queen Bea"—even to her face sometimes—sure helped. So what if her hunches were 98% correct? Her timing was usually way off. The rest of them weren't so high paced; they had lives away from her projects.

Bea sailed around the resentful in-laws, disgruntled employees, envious neighbors—but watch out. Everyone was oiling up with cocktails. Bea better be careful how much she drank. She cruised in toward those who care, or seem to—she was more susceptible to flattery than's safe for someone in her position.

Why'm I so cautious? Clare thought. *Isn't that what makes me the manager and her the genius? I sit back and worry while she's out there doing. Just like I did with Mom and all her ventures. Some took off, some didn't. Flops didn't seem to bother her, but they sure caused me some grief—and they weren't even my flops.*

At last everyone was seated. The ceremony could start. Clare wished there was room for her at the family table. Pearl was sitting up there, and Pearl wasn't half as much part of the family as Clare was. But Clare had been put in charge of the management table. Everyone at her table was obviously excited about this feast. You'd think Clare herself was the hostess the way she got so uptight about it all going well. 'Course Bea knows she can count on Clare to help; probably why she told her about the birthday jinx.

Retirement's an odd event to celebrate, Clare thought as she smiled at everybody sitting with her, then unfolded her napkin. It's sorta like a wake. You're supposed to be happy someone's gone, or going? She would've preferred a birthday party. Most folks don't care, long as there's lots to eat and drink. No one's really the center of attention for long; it's just pretend.

Dick stood up at just the right moment, Clare had to give him that: everyone was stuffed but not yet nodding or dancing off. He looked so stiff he must've forgotten to take the cardboard out of his tux shirt.

The way he cleared his throat she could tell how much he was basking in the attention. "Mother, tonight we pay tribute to you, an exceptional woman."

What a phony pause, Clare thought, supposedly for emphasis but really to give them more time to notice him—an "exceptional" man? (No way.) *Blah, blah, blah.*

Bea was beaming. It sounded to Clare like a letter of recommendation. Dick's so goddam formal, she fumed. *This is supposed to be a tribute; that's what he'll give, to the letter. Next he'll start spouting off his own resume, to show how qualified he is to take over...(If you think I'm gonna take orders from that twerp...Hell, I helped raise him. I'll quit first.)*

Why'd he stop so suddenly? she wondered. It sounded like someone had just changed the station. But he kept standing there, drinking in the applause.

Oh no, she groaned inwardly, he's introducing Bruce. Her breath caught in her throat. Bruce making a speech? Bea must've insisted he take part, stammer and all. He couldn't sit in the shadows forever, Clare guessed—just because he wasn't Bea's baby, or Jack's favorite—he needs a chance to shine. *And he does. Whoa, he's flying.*

People were smiling. The way Bea leaned forward Clare could tell she was about to protest, but just like he always could, Bruce headed her off. His voice was trembling; even though Clare knew better, she could tell people were touched by what sounded like feeling. "I want you to know what willing guinea pigs we were."

Guinea pigs!? Bea was trying not to look shocked. *Boy, he sounds so sincere,* Clare thought. *So innocent, so passive aggressive.*

"I only hope I can pass some of your spirit on—"-His voice stumbled here for the first time, "to my own children."

When Clare glanced at his two kids: *oh my: homogenized, suburbanized, sanitized, they're to Bea what a poor photocopy is to the original.*

Bruce must be pleased, she thought, at how enthusiastic the applause was— more than for Dick. *Nice guy style wins out over slick.*

Instead of calling on Corey, whose turn it was in the line-up, Dick called on John instead. *Men first?* Clare wondered. They weren't going to leave her out, were they? No one at the head table seemed to notice Clare waving. Should she speak up? Cause a scene? Or just trust John not to forget her?

John was saying something soft. Clare could hardly hear it. "Mom, I love you"?

Bea winced? She sure looked embarrassed. Too much naked feeling in front of too many people. But only those of them up front could hear him. John was tuned to her response. He stopped talking, pulled out his dulcimer (one instrument Bea never could wire to the computer) and played a song. He wrote it for Bea, Corey told Clare. *Sweet but strange. Sounds like from space.* Clare noticed that it made some people restless.

Ok, John, that's enough, she thought, *stop playing.* He seemed lost in his own world. She wished she could protect him from the titters tickling around the edges of the crowd. He looked so vulnerable, pale, like he hadn't slept in days. *Those dark rings around his eyes. As if he's talking to outer space—or from it.*

Still the baby, she thought. *Genuinely innocent. Still shields himself from everyone's else opinions, suggestions. That's how us youngest ones survive.*

When he stopped, there was silence. *Don't they know it's over? Are they rude enough not to clap?* Maybe she and Corey together could applaud loud enough for everybody. Some folks joined them. A smirk crawled across Bruce's face. *Too bad his own triumph can't make him generous enough to sympathize with John.*

Thank goodness, Clare thought, Corey's leaning over to protect John. From her expression she must be making a joke. Like kids, they couldn't stop giggling. Clare started giggling too, tension suddenly draining away.

Uh oh, she noticed, *Bea's upset. Stop grinning, you fool,* Clare told herself. *There's that dull gleam in Bea's eyes. She's reaching that point of craziness, whenever she thinks someone's making fun of her, that sends her over the edge. Good old uncle whatshisname has left his mark.*

C'mon kids, Clare shouted silently, *stop laughing. Button it up. Too late—they're out of control.* Other people were laughing too. Repressed giggles burst into snorts. *Holding laughter in makes it worse. Makes it seem ruder. Makes it seem like making fun, even when it's not. No one wants to be on the wrong side of the laughter—whether they understand the joke or not.*

Besides, Clare thought, suddenly rebellious, *we need relief from all this stiffness. C'mon, Bea, break the jinx, turn the curse into a blessing, laugh with us.*

Nope, she won't. She's too close to the edge. Now they've got to treat her very gingerly. Or else. They can't just back off. They can't just coax her out of it. It's like being a member of the bomb squad: Can we defuse this situation without too much damage?

Kids, shut up, Clare wished she could say to them. *Don't you know how left out she feels when you huddle together like that? Can't you see how upset she is?*

How could she warn them? Loudly clear her throat? Dick glanced at her for help, but Corey and John were convulsed in giggles.

And Bea was primed with too much champagne. No one else could tell, but Clare knew from the way Bea held her neck, as if her head might fall off if she moved too quickly.

Uh oh, Bea was leaning over to Pearl, muttering too loud: "Leave it to John…" She let the audience fill in the blank: to do something weird, to be a dodo, to get too emotional…?

John's eyes tightened. Corey winced, stung for him. She was more protective of his feelings than her own. Being the baby, he didn't used to get it when the boys made fun of him, when Bea put him down—but Corey did. It had happened often enough to her. Seems like as her mother's only daughter, she couldn't do anything right. When she got older, she'd jab back at the boys, be cool to her mother.

Now Corey was crumbling up her napkin, tossing it on the table. She'd been writing something on it. She folded her arms across her chest. She could be stubborn as Bea. She could sting back.

It's Corey's turn. What'll she say now? Clare wondered. *She just sits there, saying nothing.*

Dick was afraid to push the issue with Corey. But Clare could feel Bea's pressure on him.

Corey still wasn't saying anything. Everyone was staring at her. Bea was glaring. Then again she turned to Pearl. Pearl sank into her chair, dying to run off to the bathroom, Clare would guess. What Bea said was loud enough for the whole room to hear. Then she laughed. No one laughed with her.

If this was just family, Clare thought, *she wouldn't be so mean or she'd turn it into a joke; she might even apologize. But in the public eye, she freezes into an icicle, a sharp, cold distillation of herself.*

It was no secret in the family what Bea thought about the kids' financial success. *But why,* thought Clare, *does she have to go public with her private judgements? John's her heart. He's got the kind of creative genius that pulled her out of the dump (with a big boost from Jack's wallet). So what if Corey doesn't make a lot of money? What she does is a hell of a lot more valuable than Dick's wheeling and dealing. God, Bea,* Clare muttered to herself, *you measure too much by the almighty dollar.*

So why was Clare surprised by this scene? It was the public eye, the pressure was on, someone was bound to blow off steam. Ykkes, the silence was much too heavy. *They better do something before folks get nervous and bustle off without dessert or dancing.*

Dick's signaled to Jeanne. She popped up to read her tribute. *Oh, that girlish voice.* Bea interrupted her. *Oh, Bea, don't,* pleaded Clare to herself. *Let well enough alone.*

Bea's anger pulsed across the room. How she hated to be crossed. And Corey was really crossing her now. Bea couldn't just say, as she would at home, "Damn it, girl, speak up!" But she couldn't cover her rage either. *Oh no, she must be kidding!*

As she pushed the content of Bea's announcement out of her mind, Clare observed the mix of expressions on the kids' faces: shock, delight, mistrust, confusion, gratitude, skepticism, puzzlement. What lasted longest was disbelief.

Yeah, Clare knew down deep Bea didn't measure everything by dollar signs, but was she really ready to give it all up? Did she know what she was doing? Did she expect the kids to support her? It's one thing to give up control of the daily business—but was she ready to hand over ownership of the whole shebang?

Clare hoped Bea wasn't doing this in the heat of the moment—a magnanimous gesture to show Corey up as petty, childish. Was this what she'd been planning, dropping her not so subtle hints about? Clare was preparing for a shift in command, but she didn't fully get what Bea was driving at.

If Bea went, Clare must go too. They ran the business like a pair of eyes. But Clare was not ready to retire. She was only 53.

Yeah, she knew how tired Bea was of the role. She knew some other part of Bea needed to grow. But were women able to stop mothering just by telling the kids to stop calling them "Mom"? Could they step out of their shells that easily? Without something else to step into?

But Bea was not one to change like a snail. Lightning bolts were more her style.

Uh—what's this? Clare wondered as John started playing one of his instruments. Folk music. And Corey started to dance. Clare was surprised. She didn't know Corey could dance like this. How lovely—like sunshine in a storm.

These kids are brilliant, she thought—*my kids too, in a way. So skillful, so expressive. It's wonderful.*

Suddenly, in the midst of this performance, Bea stood up. *No, Bea,* Clare silently pleaded, *don't! Where are you going?...just when the kids are shining. Why can't you lighten up? Why can't you let it go? Why do you always have to be center stage?*

Trust Dick and Jane—Clare didn't care what her real name was—to march out with her. And there go Bruce and Barbara too—like a line of wooden ducks.

Clare rushed over to John and Corey, but it was too late—they'd already shrunk back into themselves, stung.

Around her Clare could hear the whispers.

"I can't believe she really means to do this."

"She was always one for the grand gesture."

"But can you imagine her ever giving up control?"

Some were chuckling.

Good grief, Clare thought. *She jinxed herself. She may be a genius, but she sure can be a dodo.*

✳   ✳   ✳   ✳

Who's Bea think she is telling me to "shut up"? When I finally told her after the party—very gently—that she'd been off the wall with the kids. What right's she got telling me it's none of my business? How dare she, at this point, tell me to butt out? When she needed me to be "part of the family," you could spread that la-te-da with a knife. Now suddenly it's all family business and I'm not a member.

For all these years, I've put my own family second and hers first. I helped raise those kids. The way she pushed and prodded and sliced and diced, it's a wonder she didn't end up with hamburger patties for children. It was me who smoothed the edges, soothed the hurt spots.

Same with the business. She was always ripping and tearing into people and things. I did all the mending. She was always dashing from one high point to another like an explorer who had ten days to discover a new continent. It was me who lingered in the valleys, felt the water running through my toes, discovered the specks of gold in her projects—and pointed them out to her when she sank low. It was my singing in the choir that turned her on to the music. It was my playing by ear but not being able to read that opened up the use of music for education (If I have her to thank for my literacy, she has me to thank for a million dollar idea.)

What a queen! Everyone revolves around her like a swarm of bees. Doesn't she just foster our dependence? She makes her will our will, her desire our desire, her satisfaction our satisfaction—and her anxieties, our anxieties. And we loved and respected her for this? What fools.

At least some of us did. What a shock she's in for when she realizes the ones who pretend to love her don't and the ones who do have been shut up.

For all her lashing out and putting down she's never before told me to shut up. Me, shut up? I hardly say anything as it is. She used to keep telling me to "Speak up!" Yeah, sure, until I tell her what she doesn't want to hear: the truth.

Well, one thing I can be grateful for: no more obligations to her and her nutty family. No more kowtowing to her. It's always no-win with her anyway. She puts everyone to shame as it is. Who could be more talented, better organized, more generous, able to balance self-interest with the common good? (Of course if her self-interest is the same as our self-interest, no problem.)

What we don't talk about is how her in-laws put her through college after their son got her pregnant or how she got the capital for the business from Pearl's insurance when her husband died and Jack's inheritance when his father died. With all that help, maybe a lot of us could be more generous, talented, and so on.

Looks like I'm not going to be a member of the family business much longer either. Dick's busy, busy, busy reorganizing the whole company. In his slimy way he's making me retirement offers I better not refuse—or get fired. He's found excuses to lay off or fire most of Bea's key people—despite my protests. Doesn't bother him the grief he's causing, the unemployment he's paying.

My days as manager are numbered. They ignore me at meetings. I comment on something, there's a pause, they keep on talking as if I weren't there. Hell, I know more about the business than all of them combined. I see why Mildred complains that everyone goes deaf when she speaks. "We old folks don't have hearing problems; young folks do: they can't hear beyond the sound of their own voices."

At least the paycheck's still coming in. Maybe Bea'll take charge again when she gets back. Queen or not, she can't just desert us without arranging for some kind of transfer of power. Dick's staging some kind of takeover.

Or should I just bow out before I get booted out? I don't want to retire. But I could never work for Dick. What's so unappealing about that guy? He was half-grown when I came along and already cocky as hell. The harder he tries to ingratiate himself with me, the more he gets on my nerves. Reminds me of that phony who sent Curtis to prison.

Guess I owe it to Bea to hang in there long enough for her to get back. With my red hair, yellow skin, thick lips and bodacious bottom—who else woulda taken me in like she did? A high school drop out, immigrant from the south with an accent thick enough to require a passport, awkward, shy—who else woulda given me that opportunity?

Besides, aren't we friends?

Then why'd she tell me to buzz off? Did the friendship last only as long as I was useful to her?

*   *   *   *

Mildred's still my friend. Else I never would've come over here for dinner. Shoulda known it'd cause a family crisis. Bruce seems extra paranoid; Barbara's of course in overdrive. As a non-family member, I sure have an insider's view on all their shenanigans, mishigosh, whatever you call it.

God only knows why Barbara and Bruce have to eek out such a meager existence (such a far cry from Dick and Jeanne's high-on-the-hog lifestyle). He's so stingy his kids can't buy new shoes until the old ones have been reheeled at least twice. And she's an expert on penny-pinching. They use economy toilet paper for just about everything: blowing noses, napkins, notes. According to Mildred, they even ration them: five squares for piss and ten for shit.

It's the Depression—or the War—all over again. What's Barbara's problem? A breach birth, hand-to-mouth survival, shuffled from one foster home to another? Just plain old poverty don't explain it; Mildred and I were both born poor and we just tssskk over this. Barbara's turned her *not having enough* into a ticket to heaven.

Whenever Mildred asks her to buy something, Barb says, "What'd you need that for?"

"I don't need it—I want it!" Mildred finally shrieked. Then she shut up. The threat of a nursing home still hangs like a loose noose around her neck. Better cool it with her "acting out." She knows how to act poor.

Barb's got a death grip on their tiny kitchen. She sniffs over the price of just about everything. She makes comments about how much food Mildred eats.

Mildred's already a bird. She can't stand eating hot dogs every night. She's losing weight, but made me promise not to tell. Another excuse for the nursing home.

This family meal, this Sunday tradition—why's Barbara trying to revive it? One more excuse to work her fingers to the bone? According to Mildred she gets up at dawn, slips off to church by herself, returns to slave piously over the stove all morning. A world class martyr. She refuses any help.

She worked herself into such a fit over whether there'd be enough food to go around, I claimed I'm on a diet. Lost my appetite by now anyway.

Bruce's head hasn't been out of the paper this whole time. Now even at the table he's hiding behind the comics. Every so often he pokes his head out to tease the kids or Mildred so they clam up even more. If he's trying to connect, it's a hell of a way to do it. If he's trying to show how superior he is, it isn't working. I used to have sympathy for this boy, but he sure is plucking my nerves now.

Now Mildred's getting upset about losing her glasses. She trying to rock the boat? Barb's caught up in the frenzy of getting the meal on the table. So Lisa—pale, pinched-faced gets the order to call over to Dick's and see if anyone there could bring the glasses on their way somewhere. No surprise—she reports sullenly that no one wanted to.

"C'mon, Gram," Bruce's voice is a little too chiding. "You're not reading or driving—what'd you need them for anyway?"

"Need? Why's everything have to be need with you? You've already reduced me to one suitcase. Even bag ladies carry around stuff they don't need. Doesn't your spirit cries out for more than just satisfaction of needs. Mine sure does."

Good question, but all he can do is wince. Silence. Mildred looks worried. Will this be her ticket to a nursing home? Barb's escaping into the kitchen, Bruce disappearing behind the paper.

"Speed's the need that prompts the greed." What's this Mildred's whispering? Doesn't look like anybody else heard her. *Speed?*

"Now, Gram," Barb's tapping Mildred on the shoulder like a parakeet. "Don't worry. As soon as we have dinner, I'll drive over and get your glasses for you." Her tone is oh so soothing, like she's talking to a baby parakeet. When she glances at me I'm overcome by a spasm of guilt for not volunteering myself. Last thing I want is facing Dick outside the office. Best I can do is nod at her generosity; she looks down with a slight smile on her careworn face.

Here comes the roast chicken. Can its skinny little legs and wings, its tiny tender breast satisfy all these appetites? What's Bruce leaping up for? Once minute lost in a pout, the next disappearing into the bathroom.

Now what? Barbara seems too busy with her chores in the kitchen to join us. Guess whatever Bruce's doing in the bathroom is going to occupy him while the food gets cold. Heck, I'm going to eat—at least pick at my meager share. These two kids are so quiet, so pale, so furtive (quite a switch from Dick and Jane's hellions). They're wolfing down their dinner like wild animals do when they've gotten into the garbage and humans are about to come out of the house with flashlights.

Of course Barb and Bruce are too distracted to pay any attention. Barb's wiping her forehead wearily, collapsing at the table finally, but only just resting before jumping up to do the dishes—doesn't anybody around here ever offer to help her? Now here's Bruce—sailing in like he's too important to bother eating. He takes a couple bites of mashed potatoes, then strolls into the living room and switches on the TV. Some high falutin' talk show—like we're too dumb to have a decent conversation with.

I've seen this stuff before. Better get into the bathroom and poke around.

Yep, sure enough. Clever—case fastened to the underside of this clothes hamper. Same old paraphernalia—mirror, straw, razor, needle. Cocaine. Curtis' needle was for heroin. Course Bruce'll never end up where Curtis is—too prominent for that.

Still, it's just as hopeless. No way anything in this house is going to get any better. Any minute now Bruce'll betray the bunch of them for another snort. Mildred's not safe here. She must not realize how dangerous it is.

Now I see why nobody offers to help. The more we do to help Barb clean up, the more work she creates for herself. If we lift a dishtowel to dry dishes, she grabs it, tosses it into the laundry, searches for a fresh one.

Now I know where all their money goes, I can feel for her stingy ways. But what she wants is sympathy, not solutions. We suggest a more efficient way—like using a sponge mop and wax instead of scrubbing the kitchen floor on her hands and knees every day. Oh no, she can't. Deaf as a post.

Way Mildred tells it, nothing she does is ever right enough. Mildred's got to do nothing or give Barb the chore of doing it over. She's as addicted to deprivation and hard work as he is to cocaine.

Those poor kids. She's so much there and he's so much not there, everyone else is frozen in place.

Ok, Bea, this is it. You better get back here and rescue Mildred…pronto. Enough cruising.

*   *   *   *

What am I doing? Rushing Mildred, who's dragging her feet, into the crossed arms of Bea. It'll probably accomplish exactly nothing. What I'll get for my trouble, if I'm lucky, is premature retirement. If I'm not lucky I won't even get my pension.

As the bumper sticker says, "I'd rather be scuba diving."

She didn't even call me when she got back from her cruise. I don't care. I'd rather be in the water than sailing on it.

Floating down there in that silent world, gliding past coral flower beds. Each creature stranger than the last, each allowed its own bright colors—including me. Discovered what a strong swimmer I am. Mom always said I was a little tadpole. I really feel at home in the water. You don't have to say anything. In fact, it's best to keep your mouth closed. All you have to worry about is bumping into something or someone. (Maybe a shark or two.) I could've stayed there forever.

Getting dumped has been good for one thing. I'm thinking a whole lot more about what I like to do, and when. Instead of adjusting to the beat of somebody else's drum, I'm following my own pleasure principles. It's fun. An ice cream sundae today, scuba diving tomorrow. Maybe retirement wouldn't be so bad after all. Used to be, when I was a kid, I knew how to have fun. Before I had a kid myself.

Could tell from Dick's questions Mildred was bound for confinement—a nursing home, if she's lucky. She's no more addled than I am. Why does she keep clowning it up? Plays the fool to avoid risking being the fool?

She's not playing the fool now. Just look at her—she could be driving this car. Doesn't miss a sight—the berry pickers, the ducks, the cupola—or a sign. A better navigator than Bea. Keeps putting everything together. What's she know she ain't telling me?

What'd I know I ain't telling myself? After how Bea's treated me, why am I doing this? Is helping her out just a bad habit? Maybe I'm trying to put her to shame by rescuing the mother she abandoned. Maybe I'm showing her what a good friend I can be even though she's been such a lousy one.

Oh, hell, I don't know. I can't let them persecute this old woman just because the family needs a scapegoat. Does every family have to have a scapegoat? Mine sure did. Glad it wasn't me.

Besides, I'd do the same for Mom if she was alive. It's just not right to stick old folks away in a closet just because old age bothers us. It's one thing if they're really sick, but Mildred is as active and lively as I am. Any family as well off as Bea's ought to take care of their own.

Wish I could've done more for my parents. They were just too proud for their own good. Lived close to the bone and liked it that way. Or so they always said. Had no use for rich folks. Almost always had enough. Trouble starts, they said, when folks have got too much. Never told them how much money I made—afraid they'd say I was stuck up. Told 'em I'd saved up to buy them that trailer. Then they turned around and gave it to Ralph and his family. Just couldn't leave that old shack. It was home. Left it only when they died.

I can see them now standing over there at the edge of that line of trees. They shrink into the woods. They fade like old photos.

When they were gone, I took to Bea's family even more. Bea's sorta like Mom. Not in terms of money, but in terms of busyness. Mom had no end of projects: the quilting, the new crops, the preserves, the church doings, the poor baskets. Dad would tease her about always having some new iron in the fire, so she kept her worries from him: shared them with me. You'd think with all her energy, she'd have more confidence in herself. She'd worry ahead of time, but by the time she got something done—and she usually did a good job, though sometimes it didn't work out—she was on to something else, some new worry. I was kinda her worry stone—being the youngest, I guess I didn't have much else to do.

Here we are. The outlaws reach the outpost. What's she gonna do when she sees us? She's had plenty of time to be angry. I'm not looking forward to one of her lashings.

She's out on the porch. She looks suspicious. She looks irritated. She thinks we're intruders.

No, she recognizes us. She smiles.

For some reason I'm remembering my dream from last night. I'd been taking care of two people who were fighting with each other. Soon as they got back together—thanks to me—they left me all alone. I had taken care of everybody else; no one was left to take care of me.

I started out grown-up and then I shrank into a kid. I ran away.

Then I was swimming. Someone hugged me from behind. I couldn't see, but I realized it was a huge fish, maybe a dolphin or a porpoise. Warm, soft, full. It felt wonderful. But when I woke up, I felt sort of ashamed.

Now I feel funny too. Like a little red potato again looking up at the glamorous Bea. But she seems different. Her eyes are softer.

She's reaching out to hug me. I guess she's not pissed anymore. I guess I'm not either.

*   *   *   *

Shots deep in the woods. So sharp, they tear the air. It's hunting season. Bea's gone for a walk. Where is she? Beige pants, green sweater—a perfect target.

This path's so hard to run up. Rocks to trip over. Roots to stumble on. The streams cuts deeper, away from the path; the earth rises. Pushing, panting, against my own gravity.

There's the waterfall—and Bea, her uncombed hair wild, a blanket wrapped around her. She looks like some ancient, pagan...I don't know—goddess? Powerful. Fragile. Beautiful like frosted leaves. Delicate like she'll shatter before the sun can warm and soften her.

She's freezing as she sees me running toward her. Without her glasses she must not know me. Does she see me as an attacker?

I better slow down. Now she recognizes me—moves toward me, into my arms. A moment to hold her close, a chance to give comfort to one who holds us all at arm's length.

"Those shots!"

"Hunters."

She's so relieved she laughs. Who'd she think was after her? Tears spring to her eyes. "What it's like to be a deer."

"Your only defenses, stillness and speed."

Together we feel safer. Back toward the waterfall. So many memories of family outings here: Jack teaching the boys how to fish, Corey talking to a frog, John wading and squealing.

"How lucky you are not to have children, Clare." Her voice, no longer bitter, sad.

What to say? Put up shreds of the old pretense? Our friendship's still tender. But I can't keep witnessing to her griefs without her knowing about mine.

"I do have a child. A son. His name's Curtis."

She's trying to cover her shock. "How old is he?"

"Thirty five.

"Then he was with you when you first came to us...Why didn't you tell me?"

"He was with my mother then. I had to send him back. I couldn't support him on my own. Then when I wanted him back, he didn't want to come, Mom didn't want to let him go. When he did finally come, it was hell on wheels."

"Where is he now?"

"In prison. He's been there awhile; he'll stay awhile longer."

"Oh, Clare, how hard."

Tears welling up. Can she understand how I feel?

On the damp rocks, close to the spray of the waterfall, I tell her the whole story: how I'd left Millersville out of pride, pregnant with no husband to show for it and no prospect of one (I couldn't shame my family that way; they were models in their church; I was a good child); how I came up here to the big city, took odd jobs to support us; couldn't make it; sent him back to Mom to live for a few years while I got on my feet; how he resented coming back to live with me; how with me working so hard and no other grownup around, I couldn't control him; how once I was making good money I tried to keep him off the streets and sent him to a better school; how the rich kids there got him into cocaine, how he turned to heroin and dealing and robbery I knew nothing about until it was too late...The whole sorry mess.

Now she knows why I never spoke of him. Shame. Took me awhile to figure out I wasn't ashamed of him but of myself. By then it was too late.

Is she still listening?

Can I tell her about the poems he wrote in prison, how he's working on his college degree, how he'll be the first in our family to graduate from college? Maybe that's the only way he could've. God works in mysterious ways. When I was eighteen and bulging—facing a tongue lashing from our minister—I didn't give a good goddam for God's ways. Now I'm willing to allow as how they might be mysterious.

Oh, those poems. Little nuggets of anger and resentment. Blaming everything on me. For abandoning him. For smothering him. Was I ever mad when he sent them! How'd he think he could get away with blaming me for everything he did wrong?

"I mean it. Do we have to be sponges for all their messes? Why should we be everybody's favorite kicking post? Just because I'm somebody's mom don't make me responsible for poverty, unemployment and the drug racket. Come off it!"

I feel funny, like suddenly I'm making a speech or something. I'm even waving my arms around. But Bea's nodding.

"So I gave him back what he gave and then some. I told him how hurt I'd been by him. I told him how disappointed I was. But when the blame and bitterness died down, we began again on new ground. We write letters. I visit him. When he gets out, I'll help him find a job, a place to live."

Bea's eyes are clouding over. She's thinking of her own kids, I bet. "John and Corey love you very much," I tell her.

Is she shaking her head out of regret or shame or anger or what? Guess I won't ask. I'm still tiptoeing around the question of blame. What comes across is her despair.

Back down the path to the cabin. Mildred's standing on the porch, looking worried, then relieved. Soon as we're closer, she sings, "I'd rather be a hunter than a deer, yes I would, I surely would—if I could."

"Would you?" Bea's tone toward her mother—though flat—is changed. No hint of contempt anymore. She listens to her more carefully now. But still without much respect.

"Neither a vapor nor a target be."

"They're such beautiful animals." Bea's cutting through Mildred's bullshit for a change.

"Neither helpful nor helpless be. But sweet and ruthless like the honey bee."

I think we're both surprised that Bea winces. But then—can't believe it—Mildred's actually stretching up to peck her on the cheek. A rare display of affection between them. Is Bea confused by it? She's turning to stare into the woods. "What's it like to be a hunter?" she asks.

"My dad was a hunter, a duck hunter. Mostly he and his buddies needed some excuse to just sit in the sun, drink beer on weekends, and watch the water flow, weaving patterns with the sunlight. Rest of the week they were working their asses off—usually for somebody else." I never much thought about him killing anything.

"Some of them, though, focus on anything with a will of its own, anything with self-propelled activity, apart from their own, and zero in on it." Yeah, I knew men like that too.

"My dad was hunted like that once," I say. "The company men—same as the sheriff in those days—were trying to throw him in jail for organizing the union. He never shot ducks after that. Said it gave him a whole new view on things."

Mildred's still playing with the idea. "We may be the hunted, but they're the haunted. When I die, I'll come back as a deer just to torture those bastards."

It's fun to giggle with Bea. "The girls," Mildred calls us.

*   *   *   *

Now that they've gone to sleep, I'm trying to write Bea a note thanking her for listening. It sounds too corny. Crumpled up in the fire, the paper burns into ashes which hold its shape—looks like a knot.

"The Murmur of a Bee
A Witchcraft—yieldeth me—
... 'Twere easier to die—
Than tell. "

—Emily Dickinson

JOHN

Youngest child of Bea and Jack, younger brother of Dick, Bruce and Corey, a musician, a disc jockey, lover of Scott.

John was delighted by the news of his mother's retirement party. Immediately he began planning how to entertain her, how to celebrate. As he rushed through Golden Gate Park on his way to work, he even skipped. Despite his pudgy appearance, he was quite agile. As he bounced along, a song from his childhood sounded in his head. *How'd it go?* he thought.

"What shall we buy at the store today?

What shall we buy, what shall we buy?" she'd sing.

"Spaghetti and ice cream pie,

Peanut butter and a magic sky," I'd reply.

"So we can chew

And we can fly," we'd tune together.

Yes, folks, he spoke to an imaginary audience, *it was not unlike growing up in an operetta. We'd sing together all the time, just me and her and sometimes maybe Bear-pooh. Running errands, humming to the rhythm of the tires. Sometimes she'd sing about her worries; sometimes I'd sing about my problems. Such as they were in those days.*

"If only the day had six more hours," she'd intone, "six more hours," and we'd chant a hundred variations of "six more hours" all the way to the store.

"My teacher is mean," I would howl, "she makes me eat Jell-O and her tongue is green."

How old was I? he thought, slowing to a walk, panting. *No more than four or five. Before I found out not every mom and boy talked things over this way. Before the big boys overheard us and started laughing at us.* The sneering faces of his older brothers intruded upon this primal scene.

Oh Mom, he cried to himself, raising his arms dramatically toward the sky, *come back to the music-making, give up the money-making. Come play with me again…*

How lucky he felt to be able walk to work through the park. How beautiful the bridge, sturdy as gold in the evening fog. "Hi, ho, hi, ho, it's off to work I go—I'll keep on singing all day long, hi, ho, hi, ho." Maybe being a disc jockey wasn't his mom's idea of a decent job, but it suited him just fine: on the air two times a week, on the stage three times, and home with his honey pie two times—what could be sweeter?

He wondered if Bea would play with him if she knew the truth about his life? *Now that she's retiring from all that buzz-buzz business*, he thought, *should I tell her?*

He gasped. A girl lay under a tree as if unconscious. Was she dead? Her body looked twisted, her hands were red. He'd better check. No, it wasn't blood, it was crimson high-heels she was clutching in her hands, perhaps for weapons, her throat wasn't slashed, she wasn't even visibly bruised. And when he peered more closely, he could see she was breathing ever so slightly. His own breath rushed out in relief.

She wasn't a girl, she was a woman, more his age, obviously in trouble, with one dilapidated suitcase and a plastic bag stuffed hastily. A refugee from a battering husband? an addict thrown out by her family? a tourist who couldn't find a hotel room? Should he help her? He'd have to wake her to ask. And what could he do for her? He had no money, they had no extra space, and what if she got the wrong idea? She didn't look well.

He glanced at the watch he carried in his pocket. *I'm late, I'm late…no time to say hello, goodbye, I'm late, I'm late, I'm late. Even when you work at night,* he thought, *you're driven by the clock.* He decided to check back on her after the program.

Maybe he shouldn't tell his mother about himself, he thought as he crossed a road against the traffic. Would she ever throw him out, disown him, as some friends' parents had? Weren't they in tune together? Or had the focus on profits drained away her creative juices?

Away from trees and back with people, he still kept humming under his breath. *Kids just naturally sing what they want to say,* he thought, *when they're happy. Not many grown-ups do.*

When he arrived in the studio, there was just enough time to hang up his jacket, grab a cup of coffee, and turn on his standard introduction: "Evening, folks, welcome to another evening of Other Worlds, Other Music, the latest in new and international music."

As his voice perked on, he leaned back and continued his reverie. Now that she was retiring, maybe she'd come visit him; she'd never been out here before. They could play music together. She could rap with his friends. He grinned. Sure, they were a weird bunch, but she would set them all a buzzing, believe thee me. He and she could improvise again.

He had some things to teach her. He could show her how to find the new rhythms, how to go into your own silence to hear them. How to let go of the programmed rhythms, the click, click, click of the gears of profit.

All you have to do, he told her in his head, *is put your ears under water in the tub and listen to your heart beat, listen to your lungs breathe in and out, play with the sound of wind through your nostrils. Then go out and tune in to breeze rippling over water, sun pulsing into your eyeballs, waves pounding onto rocks, dogs howling together, a feather stroking against your skin.*

Well, maybe not the feather, he revised. *We'll start with the heartbeat. I'll give her a drum, help her sound what she hears from within. But will she ever stop to listen?*

The tape had stopped. It was time for him to talk in real time. "Tonight, friends, a special treat: new on compact disc, a fascinating dialogue between sitar, koto, and synthesizer, the music of the Buddha Babe..."

As he switched on the music, he had an inspiration. For his mother's party. His music, Corey's dancing: Corey and the Rhythmettes (me, myself and I— though I'd love to import the Frisco Gang in full regalia). It would be a perfect way to introduce her to the rhythms.

May this retirement, he prayed to the God at the receiving end of radio waves, be the end of that public self, that shell of propriety who is Bea. And underneath may I find the Mom who will accept me for who I am. The one who sings, who harmonizes, who engages the tones, who follows the rhythms.

He resolved to call Corey as soon as he got home. He'd better talk her into this right away. He imagined her resistance. It was going to be a hard sell.

*   *   *   *

John felt relief when the plane finally took off.

It all shrinks away, he thought, watching the ground drop beneath them. Soon that void will be just a dot in time. Soon I'll be home in my own sweet life.

Mentally he shut the door on family and opened a window onto his job as a disc jockey. It didn't pay much but more than what he made as a musician, his real vocation. And he enjoyed hiding his slightly plump baby face behind the microphone. All people knew of him was his deep, resonant, slightly sophisticated, somewhat down-home voice.

What shall I play on the program tonight? he wondered. *No dear old classics as I'd planned, lost in my sentimental fog. How about something original? something special? something just for you, oh Queen of Queens. "Something by yours truly," this smooth, progressive, mellow, and oh so familiar and reassuring voice transposed to the keyboard...playing instead of talking for a change. Sure, sure, how to get bounced out on your pretty little ear.* Bounced out of his job, he was thinking, but what he was remembering was how his mother had just bumped him out of her life.

Queen of Queens and scene of scenes. *Oh Mom, how could you?* he thought. *Why would you?* He sighed as the stewardess announced the beverage selections. *Every time I return, a wider gulf. Each time I'm more a stranger, each time I've changed by a slight degree which leaps by quantitative bounds, through a Fibonacci series, increasing proportionately until it enters a whole new range of differences which cannot be told or heard: first a note, then a key, then a whole new scale.* Each time, the silence grows deeper, the music more remote, and home even stranger.

Oh course, a voice in his head reminded him, *you haven't exactly been forthcoming about who you are.* He wondered then if it was just his warped view that things had gotten much worse at home. Had his own focus sharpened with distance or had the arrogance refined its bite? Had his own outcast state shown him, at last, that unconscious sense of privilege, unchallenged superiority, insolent power, unbounded ego which could look out on bowed or nodding heads, flattering tongues, envious eyes without doubt or fear?

Bea's hands, once so tender, no longer tentative or gentle, he thought, are decisive, commanding, pointing. His brothers' hands are trapped in greed like the monkey's fist in the jar, wrapped in self-protection like boxing gloves. They've forgotten the risks of touching, of stretching, of playing. They've reached for the stars and settled for tinsel. They've spread their wings and swollen up like blimps. They've searched for harmony and turned into cacophonous one-person bands.

Oh life, he prayed, spare me such a passage. *Keep me to the lean and narrow way if such a way can save me. Let me settle for the hidden path, the back door, the shadow side of the street as long as the music keeps sounding, energy still flows, the journey is genuine.*

He accepted his ginger ale and took an appreciative sip, then set it back down. He wasn't really thirsty, but he had trouble saying no to women whose job it was to wait on people.

The plane cut through clouds and emerged into sunshine and blue sky. Please don't let me become a stranger to myself, he thought. *What a relief to be free of those strangers I thought I knew, this alien family. Only Corey, so loving, is my sister in the deep heart's core.*

He thought of his lover, who would be waiting for him at the airport. *What joy to be flying back to the one I love, my darling companion, you who know me best. Hearing your voice on the phone, my heart both leaps and rests. Wait for me, wait, I'm coming, I'm coming, into your arms, dear one.*

He wiped a tear from his left eye. Away from this nest of blind eagles and deaf vipers.

He let the past fall back behind him, beneath the cloud cover, and looked out to the distant horizon.

What a shame they'll never know you. Never know all the reasons I love you: your tenderness, your wit, your quirks, your gifts.

*   *   *   *

This homelessness feels right. Matches my empty inside with an empty out. Leaving me only this sterile room where they've confined me.

No home but this box to hide in, this cage for my despair. They've isolated me here, I can feel it. No ward for pneumonia patients, this hole for the dying, this dungeon. Better out under a tree in the park.

Better to drift as a leaf in a careless wind, roll as a can in the gutter, slink as a stray alley cat. Truer that a prodigal son has no home to return to, no welcoming arms to deceive him into believing the world has not betrayed him at the end.

The end? Am I going to die?

"This world is not our home; we cannot tarry here." Now not the new but the old songs come. If not here, where? Where can we tarry? What does it mean to have a home? I've never been able to provide a home for myself—I've had rooms, apartments, even a house, but never a home just for me.

When a lover leaves you, when you lose a friend, you rattle around in the empty space like a dried up pod, crushed by vacant stares, those blank mirrors around you, which cannot, will not, reflect your grief.

Oh, Scott, forgive me for leaving you like this. I couldn't take the risk of staying. Not now that we know what we know. I just couldn't bear to be that burden, the revelation of your own possible decline.

Were I a saint, considering the lilies of the field, or a wandering sadhu, trusting the generosity of strangers, this body alone would be home enough for me. But it feels emptier and emptier, a ghost town.

My throat tightens, caught between my heart and a hard place. I feel like music without a song to sing, without a melody's shape, without the shelter of chords, without instruments to sound me, a key to enter by, or an ear to rest within.

Where once was a mother to shield me, a friend to play with, a lover to resonate for, is now echo, then silence.

Thank god—oh, god, are you who I used to hear in the music?-Soon Corey will come to protect me from this emptiness. It's expanding me like a vanishing cloud. Nothing to hold onto but the cold frame of this bed.

Many connections have been severed in this place, flesh cut and bones broken. You can feel violence in the air, rising up out of the antiseptic blankness, anger bouncing off the tight walls, futility pressing down with the low ceilings, alienation enforced by the few squinty windows…up high and trapped like people in the projects. But this is supposed to be a hospital, a healing place. That doctor knows. He nodded when I said where I was from. He asked me who I lived with.

I must not stay here long.

If I go soon, I want room to fly away on wings of light, fluttering a song of praise.

Meanwhile, thanks dear sister, I know you'll come to me soon. Already I curl into the core of your loving heart and listen to the wind outside, howling.

If I had energy, I'd howl too. I'd howl against this eviction being forced upon us—my friends, my lovers, my chosen brothers, and me. We did not choose this scourge, we do not deserve it. And don't think for a moment by sticking us into these back rooms, hiding us in your cellars, you can escape this plague. It may be our brand, but malignancy does not discriminate.

Scott, my darling, please be spared. Resist the eviction.

You can wander the streets only so long before the emptiness collapses in on you, like a closet, like a cell, like a black hole.

Black holes, they're saying now, are where galaxies are born. May one star, in the galaxy emerging from this black hole we're lost within, be named for me.

I sleep, I wake, blurred the boundary between, dreaming, remembering all the same.

Nothing to read when I'm awake but this bible, left here by the last, late? occupant…snatches of truth:

> *The mouth of the wicked and the mouth of the deceitful are opened against me; they have spoken against me with a lying tongue. For my love they are my adversaries. Because these men remembered not to show mercy, but persecuted the poor and needy, because they clothed themselves with cursing, let it come into their loins like oil, like water into their bones. Let mine adversaries be clothed with shame.*
>
> *My god, my god, why hast thou forsaken me? I am despised of the people, but thou art he that took me out of the womb; thou didst make me hope when I was upon my mother's breasts.*
>
> *My heart is like wax; it is melted in the midst of my bowels. My strength is dried up like a potsherd; and my tongue cleaveth to my jaws; and thou has brought me into the dust of death. My loins are filled with a loathsome disease and there is no soundness in my flesh. I am gone like the shadow when it declineth.*

My heart panteth, my strength faileth me; as for the light of mine eyes, it also is gone from me. My lovers and my friends stand aloof from my sore; and my kinsmen stand afar off.

Oh that I had wings like a dove! for then would I fly away and be at rest. And there I would praise the Lord with harp; sing unto him with the psaltery and an instrument of ten strings. Sing unto him a new song; play skillfully with a loud noise.

Who wrote this? Someone way back then understood—why don't they understand now?

*   *   *   *

After the wolf carried me away, after the wolf carried me away in her mouth, away from the furry nest, away from the rocky ground where I fell, after the wolf took me from them, I cried out.

I cried for his sturdy back, I cried for his soft signals, his gentle nuzzling, his generous mouth. I cried for her wet fullness, I cried for her rough tongue, her warm softness, I cried. The wolf didn't care. The wolf carried me without glancing back, without stumbling, without tearing me, into the desert and dropped me there.

There in the vast emptiness, there on the burning sand, there my throat dried up, my skin turned purple, and every move ached. There she left me, without biting me, without licking me, without either desire or tenderness and there I lay, trembling.

Trembling in that heat, chilled inside, seared outside, waiting for the first vulture to sense me, the first owl to spot me, the first coyote to track me. Waiting without hope for them to find me.

But find me she has. I lean into her soft fullness, she strokes my fur, my fever drains into her coolness, her warmth absorbs my chills, her calm stills my shivers, I am back in the furry nest. He's gone, but in the darkness I hear him calling. Soon I'll follow.

Now I rest.

"Could—I do more—for Thee—
Wert Thou a Bumble Bee—
Since for the Queen, have I—
Naught but Bouquet?"
—Emily Dickinson

COREY

Only daughter of Bea and Jack, younger sister of Dick and Bruce, older sister of John, a middle school science teacher.

Well, I don't know, Corey thought as she watched her pupils enter the solar system. Some zipped around their circles, while others painstakingly traversed each globe their pencil produced. *Indulging John's whimsy is appealing; making a total fool of myself has less of a draw.*

As she stood there quietly, her loose brown hair tied back to imitate a school-marm, she seemed more subdued than she really was. The only thing she didn't like about being a teacher was having to dress the part: skirt, stockings, bra. The kids could care less; it was for the sake of other teachers and administrators, many of whom were as resistant as she was to looking so respectable. Sometimes she felt like turning cartwheels, but because she was short and thin, it behooved her to behave like an adult lest she be confused for one of her students.

In this context it was fun to imagine dancing at her mother's retirement, as her brother was proposing. He's right. Dancing might be one way of communicating novel enough to get Mom's attention. Does she remember when we used to dance together? She used to pick us both up and whirl around. Later she taught us the Charleston and the Lindy and the Samba. But mostly we just twisted and bounced, each one alone but all together. It was fun, it just seemed so natural—until it stopped. We got too old or she got too busy, I don't remember which.

The faster kids were getting restless.

"Ok, class, now that you've drawn your suns, please draw the planets. Does everyone remember what a planet is?" From the puzzled, excessively pleasant expressions and furtive glances at other people's papers, she guessed that everyone didn't. She hated asking these questions where the kids knew she already knew the answer: *What is a planet?* But she knew if she just told them over and over, they'd never learn. "What do you know about planets?...That's right, they revolve around the sun…Yes, our earth is a planet too…Very good, Joey, in the right order too."

Why didn't the girls ever volunteer? She worried whether she favored the boys somehow.

Mom seems to listen to the boys, she thought. *She never seems to hear me. Sometimes she gets the facts straight and she likes to tell her friends I'm a science teacher. Hard to do anything she hasn't already done; science at least gives teaching a new twist. But then when I tell her stuff I'm really excited about, like the Blue Nova, she's a million miles away. Her eyes glaze over and I end up talking to myself.*

Joey finished his solar system and started sketching in other galaxies. Some of these kids didn't know where Kentucky was while others were ready to give her eyewitness accounts of the births and deaths of Supernovas.

Sometimes, Corey thought, *I feel like shouting at her,* "Hey listen to me; I've got something to say too; just because I'm a girl doesn't make me a dummy. You were a girl once too." Of course Bea was the oldest, the brightest, the best of the seven children.

Corey remembered when they visited Aunt Millie and Uncle Tim. They lived in an old farmhouse that'd been in his family for years, most of the rooms shut off. Wood stove in the kitchen, their bed in the dining room, stacks of magazines for insulation, two old neckties around his waist for a belt. Uncle Tim let John drive the tractor and showed Corey how to slide her hand under the chickens to find eggs. The boys helped him round up a loose goat and their dad was interested to see how they planted their potatoes. Aunt Millie had about a million cats and introduced them to everything in her garden as if they were little people. And at night while they watched the stars, she gossiped about them, not just naming the constellations but telling all the old stories about them too.

Corey thought they were fabulous people, but Bea got all uptight and sharp-tongued with Millie—maybe that's how she always treated her younger sister, Corey didn't know—and afterwards she complained about the "squalor."

Corey whispered to her father, "What's squalor?" and he whispered back, "Dirt and poverty." Their home was as scrubbed as any she'd seen and they had piles of wonderful food for everybody to eat. Millie teased Tim about his makeshift belt—kind of embarrassed in front of them—and he joked back that at least it wasn't the rope he used to tie up the calf.

It was recess time. "Walk, don't run." This part of teaching was just like parenting: control, control. *Can Mom retire from being a mother?* Corey wondered. *If that's possible, I might be more eager to become one.*

She wandered out to the playground with the kids, standing in the shadows in case somebody fell down or others started fighting.

Maybe she'll relax more if she retires, Corey thought. She used to be more fun when she relaxed. Like that time we played with the box—vacationing in some mountain cabin—far more "squalid" than Millie's farmhouse—Mom called it "rustic"—too cold to swim, the fish weren't biting, everyone bored. It seemed like, after all our separate activities, we were having trouble getting to know each other again, including Mom and Dad.

Then, she recalled, *John and I found that big—and I mean "big," big enough for a grownup to get into—cardboard box.* She talked him into climbing into it and then she pushed it down the hill. She remembered how it slid real easy on the grass and he plopped out at the bottom. He loved it. Then she tried riding in it. It was just the right balance of scary—mostly 'cause you couldn't see where you were going—and exciting.

Then Bruce tried it, a little ashamed to be having so much fun with the little kids. And finally even stuffy old Dick, who must've been a teenager by then, climbed aboard. Then Mom and Dad came out to see what the squealing was all about and they talked Mom into climbing aboard. Corey was surprised at how willing Bea was. She loved it. At the end she coaxed and teased and prodded Dad into the box too. It was the coolest thing. They were laughing so hard it almost hurt.

Corey'd never been fond of boxes, ever since her father took his mother's body East in a box on the train, she just kept thinking of Mama shut up in there, unable to breathe. But this time they won over the void of the box; they filled it with life.

She watched the girls negotiate a disagreement over hopscotch rules. Some of these kids learn more at recess than they do in the classroom, she thought, wondering if she could make up a planets game that would teach them the solar system for life. Maybe they could take turns playing the sun, circling while everybody else rotated around them.

Then, she recalled, we'd had that campfire and sang songs together. Bea told stories about her childhood that weren't the usual gloomy tales of deprivation and responsibility. About sneaking into a public swimming pool at midnight and almost getting caught; about cutting off all Millie's hair so Gram had to dress her as a boy until it grew out; about making costumes for everyone out of their grandmother's old clothes and charging for showings. It had been a relief for Corey to get a glimpse of Bea's mischievous side.

How's Mom going to retire from holding the family together? Corey wondered now. *I sure hope she doesn't expect me to step into her shoes. No way I'm able to hold this family together. The oomph's gone out of her since Dad died. I thought our grief would bring us together, but she got busier than ever. What will become of us when she lets go? Of course, she also keeps us apart in a way, we're all so busy competing for her attention, her approval, her love.*

It was time to clap the children in again. At moments like these Corey felt like a jail guard.

As she waited for the stragglers, Corey figured she better decide about the dancing, call John tonight. For all his praises, she wasn't sure she could risk it in front of the assembled multitude. *Why does Mom have to go so public with our private times?* she wondered.

She smiled at Shirley skipping in late.

Oh, sometimes I just hate going home, she sighed. *The silence drops over me like a shroud. I hop off the plane my good old open, sharing and caring self, and by the time I step through the front door, the shutdown is almost total. It's like having lockjaw. To think the family used to call me "Miss Blabbermouth." But for all they cared, I might as well been born without a tongue.*

Sometimes John listened, sometimes her father heard her, if she wasn't too emotional—if she was, he shied away, leaving her feeling slightly hysterical. Bea didn't want to be bothered with the feelings and she often ignored the content.

Corey stretched into her role again. "Ok, kids, let's get back to earth. Who knows the difference between a toad and a frog?"

✳   ✳   ✳   ✳

Rising, falling, this is torture. Rising, falling, this is torture. Watching your breath all day, watching your thoughts repeat themselves over and over, this is torture.

She set us up, set us up. "Ok, sweetie, open wide!" Then SMACK. Shoulda seen it coming. Mom at her worst.

Hey, Mom—huh? First she's your mom, then she's not. You're a sweet babe, then you're a knot. She does her best, then she's for naught. You're a good kid, then you're naughty. Is one times zero one—or nothing? This world is one big orphanage where everyone is crying "Mama!" and everyone replies, "Not me, kid."

This retreat was a good idea: time to think—no, not "think," watch my breath—about Clare's letter. Not to act, just watch how I react.

Can't you just see Mom's grand arrival home from her cruise—only to find the chaos that's been brewing since she left? Dick and Jeanne taking over the house, Dick taking charge of the business, Gram deported to Bruce's. Not sure why Clare's so worried about her safety there. What could harm her except straining herself trying to outmartyr Barb? Can't imagine Gram being that stupid.

Just one glance and Mom grokked the scene, headed for the woods. Her fury must've been white-hot, not just the searing anger at the party—because instead of setting things straight, she took off again. Fine with me, but not with the rest of them who feel left in the lurch: Clare, under Dick's thumb on the job, Mildred at Bruce's mercy at home.

Wonder how long Mom plans to camp out at the cabin. Might be a bit too rustic for her. I get the feeling Clare wants me to come home and rescue Mildred. And then what? I can't bring Gram back to my place—she'd die of boredom.

Rising, falling, rising, falling, in, out, in, out. Whew. I can't really blame Bea for fleeing. She's like some generator with everyone plugged into her—'cept me and John. Our disconnection from her is one good thing to come out of that fiasco.

No way I'll ever put myself in that position. She'd come into the kitchen late at night pale as the glass of milk she was pouring for herself. I wanted to relieve the pressure, but she thrives on it. Busyness is her reason for being. Rising, falling, rising, falling.

I guess I should've said something nice about her at the party. It was the perfect chance to show how much I care. But I was pissed as hell. No matter how well I know what a monster she can be, it always catches me off guard. Besides, declaring my innermost feelings to a crowd of strangers isn't exactly my style. What pleases her terrifies me. What a phony "photo opportunity." But telling her face to face wouldn't work either; she'll joke it off or dismiss it with a flip of her hand, leaving you feeling like a drooling toddler. Poor John. Look what happened to him.

Rising, falling, boy, my mind sure wanders. Rising, falling, coming back to the breath is a relief.

Yes, it's a far, far better thing for me to do than I have ever done not to sacrifice myself to the madness—to do nothing instead, to sit here watching my breath rising, falling than to rush into Mom's shoes so I can rescue everybody. From what? Who needs that system perpetuated? I don't like queens; I sure don't want to become one. Let's find a better way. Let crowns grow into hula-hoops; let everyone have one.

Let Bea discover a new energy system: not the master generator producing energy for all the dependent appliances, but the hologram: each one its own energy system, each one a whole and part of the whole. Stars in a galaxy. Rising, falling.

We are made of stardust. The oxygen we breathe, the calcium in our bones, the iron in our blood are all generated by stars. We've inherited our stardust from the millions of stars that lived and died in our galaxy before we were born.

All the mysteries of the universe, they say, are contained in this space between the rising and falling breath, the moment before it starts to rise, the moment before it starts to fall.

Once upon a time there was a powerful queen whose fame spread far and wide. Her rule was gentle but firm, strict but fair, kind but challenging. Her beauty was dazzling, her brilliance obvious, her accomplishments of benefit to all. Her realm thrived and all around her participated in that prosperity. But one day she packed up her personal belongings and left her power, her throne, her wealth behind. She went into a huge forest to live simply. When her people mourned her departure and begged her to return, she replied, "It's high time you learned to survive without me. I have cared too much for you. Don't worry. You can take care of yourselves and each other. You don't really need me."

"But why are you abandoning us?"

"I seek a higher way," she explained. They didn't understand. What could be higher than being a queen?

Rising, falling. Whose baby face keeps rising? My own baby photos? No, this one's got dark, curly hair and she (?) is cooing. Not any baby I know, but somehow familiar. Holy smokes, the babe who'll never be? The child I refused to have? But it was barely a seed when I nipped it in the bud. When we planted gardens in grade school, so few seeds actually germinated, and fewer still survived. Mrs. Chisholm said nature is really generous, allowing more than enough, providing for mistakes and failures.

I was barely out of virginity, two shots past to be exact. Fertility runs rampant in this family. But if ever a boy was not ready to settle down and raise a kid; if ever there was a boy I was not ready to settle down with. Marriage was absurd; I barely knew him. All I wanted was to find out what it felt like and he was the cutest boy I'd ever seen. That dark curly hair. I don't care if Mom and Gram both did it; I wasn't ready to be a parent at 18; I'm not ready now; I'm not sure I'll ever be. Rising/falling.

All that fussing over and minding their manners and warning them against the world out there and controlling and containing and sprucing up and nagging and

worrying about and being invested in and putting one's foot down and reading
the riot act and pleading and cajoling and manipulating and placating and standing no nonsense and making them make themselves useful and words of advice
and coaching and strong arming and being hard-boiled and tough love and keeping in line and humoring and coddling and spoiling and pampering and indulging and binding and clamping down on and being bound to and being
accountable for—all that chronic codependency.

I've got to give her credit though; Mom was great about the abortion. I'm
amazed I even told her. But in those days, I guess, I still confided in her. As soon
as it was clear to her I didn't want the baby, she didn't argue, she didn't scold;
instead she set up an appointment. It was over before I even started to have
morning sickness, no worse than bad cramps during my period, and I was a free
woman, though not as free as before I got pregnant, never again as free as that.

It was just between the two of us. No one else ever knew, not even Dad. Of
course, now I'm not sure her efficiency was motivated by compassion or by propriety: quick, before the telltale bulge. Still, I'm grateful. I was such a dodo in
those days.

Rising, falling, what if Mildred's not safe? Who's there to protect her? The
boys won't protect her. I know they won't. What should I do? To the rescue?

Rising, falling. They're pulling up my dress and poking their fingers into me.
The big boys smoking cigars in the boiler room. I wandered down there looking
for Sandy. I didn't hear them. Why are they doing this? They look mean. One of
them is laughing. It hurts. I'm ashamed, but I'm too scared to run away. They're
holding me tight. Someone's hand is bruising my wrist. Please let this be over
soon. Let me be out of here.

Back behind their panting faces, I see his eyes. Watching. He'll rescue me! No,
he's scared of the big boys. He backs out, still watching, his eyes guarded. My
own brother and he let them do it to me. He just watched. Pretended it never
happened. Never told. Forgot.

Rising, falling…falling.

*   *   *   *

Sure is a long corridor. Looks like this ward's being renovated—drop cloths,
sheetrock, ladders, paint cans. No patients. Why is John way down here?

This nurse sounds sympathetic, but obviously overworked. Sounds like John's
an extra burden. She says he's quarantined, but doesn't know why. I'm just as
puzzled as she is.

He brightens when he sees me. But he's too weak to get out of bed. Looks awful—so skinny, so splotchy, hair standing up that way. Tears in his eyes he's so glad to see me. Tears in mine too.

All I can do is hold his hand awhile.

"Corey, I want to tell you something."

Does he have something worse than pneumonia? What's he going to say?

"I'm gay."

Oh. No surprise. But funny talking about sex. I don't know what to say. I never told him about my abortion. "Are you?"

"Well?" He looks a little shaken. He must need some reassurance. "Oh, that's ok with me—I mean, you don't need my approval, do you?"

His face really changes when he laughs.

"Really, I don't have any problem with it. I never liked any of your girlfriends anyway. Do you have a lover?"

He's telling me about Scott—large family, middle child, lost mother at six, close to father, father crippled in some industrial accident, musician, actor, college drop out, came out at sixteen, fun, considerate. "He's different from some guys—he really listens, he really cares."

"Wish I knew someone like that who's straight. Sounds like someone I wouldn't mind meeting." Teasing's helpful.

"You will—but not now. I've got to get better first."

His illness...passes between us like a shadow. How sick is he?

"It's just pneumonia," he reassures me.

"Are you going to tell Mom you're gay?"

"I guess so. What do you think she'll say?"

All I can do is shrug. My best case scenario is not positive. If she hit the ceiling just because we giggled at her retirement party, imagine how she'll respond to this, the ultimate public shame.

"Well, whatever her reaction, I want to see her. Our last parting was wrenching—in fact, I never even said goodbye to her. It's time to mend that—or at least try."

"I'll get in touch with her. I guess she's still at the cabin." I can tell from the way he shakes his head he's as puzzled as I am about that development.

I dread being the messenger. Off with my head. Not enough that my tongue has already been cut out. But John's her heart. He brings out that tiny streak of tenderness she usually keeps so well hidden.

At the desk in the hospital's main lobby is a note from Dick announcing that he's made a reservation for me at the hotel across the street, so I can have easy access to John. It brings me immediately to a boiling point. Not only has he already shoved John and his germs into oblivion, but now he's going to lock me in some closet too. What right does he have to keep us out of our own house? (A flash of Mom's predicament.)

None of them have visited John since he was admitted to the hospital. Someone sent a bouquet of flowers. Turns out to be Scott. Those multicolored blooms are the only hint of life in that dismal room, aside from John's wilted face.

Leaving my bag in the hotel, I take a taxi to the old homestead. No one answers the bell so I go around to the back door and knock forever. Still no answer. Back at the front door, about to write Dick a note, I'm suddenly struck by a bolt of memory.

The time he held my head under water in the swimming pool. I'd begun to travel down that long dark tunnel. He must've got scared because he let me up. By then I'd practically forgotten how to breathe. He covered up by pretending he'd just rescued me from drowning. Quite the hero.

It wasn't fair. I was only four at the time. I hadn't done anything to him. But he always seemed to resent John and me—from the day we were born. I tried to protect John. Sometimes Dick would twist our arms so hard behind our backs, we'd scream. But it was worse if we told Mom.

It doesn't surprise me he's moved into the jolly old homestead. He always coveted it, ever since he found out Mom wasn't going to send John away to prep school like she sent him.

Let me scan his note again—is there any suggestion of compassion for John? No, it's cold, cold, hypocritically cold—and signed "love."

Suddenly furious, I can't help yelling, "You prick!" and leaning on the doorbell. Dashing out into the immaculate lawn, I grab a huge decorator stone strangling one of the rose bushes and hurl it through a bedroom window. "Take that, you bastard, creep, hypocrite, liar, thief, no good son of a lizard and a toad."

Feeling purged, I sit on the stoop and sing a song John and I love: "Hey ho, nobody home. No eat, no drink, no money have I none. But still I will be merry."

Should I seek refuge at Bruce's. No, Bruce is afraid of Dick, one of the big boys. He'll just stare at me, then turn away. Deny he ever saw me.

After visiting John again, to cheer him up with tales of my exploits and a duet of "Hey ho," I go back to the hotel.

Figuring John might be better off in a nursing home, in case he gets sicker, I call all the nursing homes in town. Most of them are full. Finally I get one with an opening. But my voice staggers at the cost.

"How sick is your brother?" asks the woman's voice on the other end. "Is he dying?" My chest tightens. What's she talking about?

"No," I cry out. "No, he's not—and he's not going to."

"Well," she says, "unless you can afford to pay a whole lot, you might be better off caring for him at home then. I could give you the name of a nurse who might be willing to come in and help."

Home? Back to point zero.

In the hotel room, I stare at the phone, unable to call Mom. True, I don't have a number for the cabin, but I could have asked around. I could call Clare or Pearl. I'm numb with fear. Is it really just pneumonia? I'm damned if I call and damned if I don't. I don't like figuring this out all by myself. I take a nap instead.

I dream I've come home and found the house full of strangers. The hub of activity is my room. When I confront Mom about why this happened without my being told or asked, she's very blase about it, says my brother (John? Dick?) was supposed to tell me.

I get so angry I rip her blouse off, yelling, "How would you like it if somebody took away your clothes?" I guess I figure our house is as important to us as her clothes are to her. But she just shrugs and says, "I could take it." Suddenly I realize, in the next scene, that she's about to parade naked through all these strangers. I'm shocked. Mom? But I also don't quite believe it. Sure enough, when I peek out, she has her slip on. But still with that protection, she looks vulnerable.

Even when I wake up, I'm still furious at her. Yes, she's the main generator, at the controls, turning us off and turning us on at her will. All the power's hers, always has been. True, she makes connections, she allows some energy to flow between us, but she could also just as arbitrarily cut off the current, shut down the light, black us out. Sure it drained her, left her burnt out—but it turned us into passive sockets.

"What's a transformer?" I ask my star pupil Joey in my head, desperate to transcend this electrical image.

Now that I feel how angry I am at her, I can see why I'm so reluctant to ask for her help. But that shouldn't stop me from finding her for John soon as possible. But how? What if the cabin doesn't have a phone? I don't have a car, can't afford a cab that far. Who could help me?

No answer at Clare's. Where's Gram? Don't want to call Bruce's. Better try Pearl. It's Opal's voice. She agrees to let me borrow her car.

*   *   *   *

Finally he's asleep. His coughing's died down. Soon Mom'll be here to take over the watch. Why isn't he getting better? Pneumonia shouldn't hang on like this. Why isn't the medicine working? That doctor's so squirmy. Won't let us take him home. But we're afraid to leave him alone. The nurses are too far away. Why won't they tell us why he's being quarantined?

I can't believe how much Mom's changed. Like the Wizard of Oz when Toto pulled back the curtain: no longer The One, but one of us. But somehow, I can't figure out how, she's more powerful than ever. Dick was practically begging her to move back into the house, but she didn't want to, decided to stay close to John.

She's listening to me. And, ironically, I find myself tongue-tied. But that first night, the night we drove back from the cabin, maybe trying to close the gap between us, I told her about the blue nova, how we are all stardust. I even sang that song, "We are stardust, billion old carbon." She liked it. Dust, she nodded, and stars: "Both."

Suddenly—briefly—I opened up; I wasn't at that moment scared of her. Before the crisis set in and we lost each other again.

She told me about her time in the woods, being on her own, the animals, the deer, the baby raccoon. She was like a stranger but someone I liked.

Now his breathing seems ok. Sounds like my car—stalling, then starting again.

John got such a raw deal being a man. Men and meanness somehow seem trapped together. Most of them never really learn how to play. They "toy" with guns; they're always trying to beat each other at something. John, the exception, the sacrifice, the one who chose the other way, the despised way of the feminine. Macho or wimp: damned if they do, damned if they don't. Stuck on the outs; maybe out there they're insiders, but the space seems hollow, without warmth, comfort, or deep sharing.

Whose fault is it? Who knows? Maybe blame isn't the issue.

His breathing's changed. What's happening? Is it the medicine or the sickness? Oh god, I hate this feeling responsible but not knowing enough to do anything to help. Mom, where are you?

His breathing's labored, but he's still asleep. Maybe I better get behind him and give some support so his lungs don't fill up with fluid. Oh, he's so heavy. If only I could pick him up. There was a time when I could pick him up as a baby.

If only I could carry him away from here, protect him. His weight's too much. All I can do is hold him, shelter him.

So soon he was a toddler, squirming out of my grasp, scrambling away, a shout of glee, my hands too small to hold him.

Oh god, he's a rock, he's pressing me down, I can't hold him any longer.

A dark cave—wings, full of light, press me back. I feel like I'm falling. I feel like I'm the rock.

His hands are turning blue. His chest rises with a long sigh, something lifts from him, light like a leaf blown by wind, and falls down again—not as heavy as before, more like clothes drifting down to the floor after you've taken them off.

My god, what's happening?

No, no, not now. It's too soon. Not before Mom comes back. No, John, no. Your hand in mine's still warm.

I'll hold you still and wait for Mom.

Should I call the nurse? I know he's gone. I almost saw him at the door, turning to blow me a kiss.

I better call her. Maybe they can bring him back. With their awful machines? Maybe he doesn't want to come back. It might only get worse. Maybe he wants to fly away. I better call.

"There is a flower that Bees prefer—
...Her Public—be the Noon—
Her Providence—the Sun—
Her Progress—by the Bee proclaimed—
In sovereign—Swerveless Tune—

...Surrendering—the last—
Nor even of Defeat—aware—
When cancelled by the Frost—"

—Emily Dickinson

MILDRED

Mother of Bea, Tom, Sally, Fred, Jason, Kathy, and Millie; Wife of Art, Grandmother of Dick, Bruce, Corey and John, and others; Great Grandmother of Todd, Angela, Cassie, Lisa, Larry and others.

Mildred had retreated back behind the garden under her favorite apple tree where the family ruckus couldn't touch her and she was free to worry about the extended family for which she was, technically, still the matriarch. She thought about her children, Bea, Tom, Sally, Fred, Jason, Kathy, and Millie; her grandchildren, Dick, Bruce, Corey, John, Sam, Margaret, Alice, Jane, Helen, Bob, Hank, Fred Jr.; her great grandchildren, Todd, Angela, Cassie, Lisa, Larry, Bobby, Freddie, Jackie, Jeanne, Mary, Kate, Sandy, Maggie, Tillie—quite a crew.

And as the sun warmed her face, she stretched out her long legs, still sturdy, stretched back her thin arms and arched her wiry body. Her handsome, weathered face might show marks of her struggles, but at her age she felt pretty good. She'd come a long way in one lifetime and she intended to go on for a while longer. She just hoped that Bea's current decision wouldn't throw a wrench in her plans.

Used to be when I was little, she thought to herself, *beyond time for the youngsters, not so long ago for me—Ma put me in charge of the chickens. I fed 'em, watered 'em, buried 'em—when the eggs were too big and they ruptured—I collected eggs, candled them, boxed them—and helped some of them brood into chicks; I released the rooster and rounded him up again; I caught and caged chickens bound for market and waved goodbye as they rattled down the dirt road on the back of the truck.*

With a smile she recalled one of the first times she put her little hand underneath a feathery tummy and started to steal the egg, the chicken pecked her hand and she grabbed the egg so tight, it cracked and got her and the chicken and the nest all gooey.

She'd thought a lot about eggs since then—how fragile they are, how you can see right through them when you hold them up to the light, and yet how sturdy, how you can roll them around and boil them in water and they still hold together. How they're a whole in themselves and yet contain new life, how the egg you eat is just as real (and just as tasty) as the chicken which could hatch from it, how the egg produces the chicken which produces the egg which produces the chicken which produces the egg and so on, around and around—of course it doesn't matter and no one can say which comes first.

'Course with all those children I had, she told herself, *I kept thinking about eggs—how I seemed to have no end of them, and what a chicken I was, never able to say no—if there's one thing I've learned while getting older, it's how to say no—not being able to gives the lie to all your yesses. But I still can't say which comes first, mother or child. When you're a child, seems mothers always come first; when you're a mother, seems the kids are always coming first.*

When I was little, she thought, shifting into the leafy shade, *Ma ruled the roost except when Pa was home, and then for those brief shining moments, he was the prince, a knight in shining armor, the last of the big time spenders, the salesman in the shiny car who left his fingerprints on all the glasses, and other places too. Pa Prince, Paw Prints. Everything shifted when he was home—like suddenly the sun started revolving around the earth at breakneck speed—and when he left, a few days later, the sun stopped, the earth moved steadily for another month or two until he tootled through again.*

That was all the change her world then held—and that was plenty—until the kids figured out there was something else—growing up. *Seemed the bigger we grew,* she thought, *the smaller Ma became—made me feel guilty. Just because I had kids, I didn't want to push her into having to be a grandma. I wanted to catch up with her—be her equal—but she just kept fading into something else. I didn't want to imitate her life, I wanted to match it with my own, but I couldn't, I fell into the same old pattern, had too many children, an absent husband (when he was drinking, he was really gone—worse than Pa's never really being there), nothing for myself—and I never caught up with her. She died first. What about when I die—will she be there waiting, unchanged? Wouldn't that be a sorry state? We're really whomped either way—if we change and if we don't.*

And now what about this retirement of Bea's? What would that do to Mildred? She was sorry to be so self-centered about this, but where did that leave her—at death's doorstep? She wasn't ready to die. *If I had my druthers*, she thought, *I'd let Bea catch up with me. Makes no never mind to me. She's already passed me by in the ways of the world: education, money, steady husband, career. Course I never retired, never did anything so grand as that, just sort of gave up, just sort of ran out of steam, just sort of quit. Suddenly occurred to me I was running on empty, nobody needed me, really needed me, anymore and I was just busy-bodying around out of habit. Still felt guilty as hell, but nobody much noticed and if they did, they put it down to my being crotchety. Life let me just sort of ease into retirement, instead of all this fal-de-rol.*

Bea was always keen on parties. *One year*, Mildred thought, *I was a slab of meat on the operating table in the morning and home in the afternoon whipping up a cake to make her a birthday party. They cut a tumor out of my breast, after knocking me out cold, then sent me home to recuperate. Felt so good the tumor was harmless, I didn't mind a little celebration. Art, of course, messed it up some way or another, as he usually did. That guy sure didn't like birthday parties—but he sure didn't mind whooping it up down at the bar. Why'd I stick with him so long? I didn't want a marriage like Ma had? I wanted my kids to know their father? Who knows? Anyway, that's water under the bridge.*

She rubbed her face in her hands and cracked her aching knuckles while her mind circled back over more immediate concerns. What's Bea up to with this retirement business? Is she cracking open her own egg, wrenching herself away from all she's known so she can fall into something new? *Only this time she hasn't got my hands or Jack's arms to fall into like when she was born or when she got married. If you ask me—and I know nobody did—she's heading for a shock.*

Bea, she figured, thinks she was just wearing a mask—cause that's what it feels like once you figure out what it is—and when she rips it off, people will suddenly know her for who she really is, will love and care for her personally and forget about everything she does for them. And they should—but they won't. Poor kid, she's gonna be disappointed. That mask is a kind of reversed mirror; when she takes it off, most people, when they can't see themselves any longer, will see nothing.

Nothing is what she'll fall into, I'm afraid. Happened to me. Nothing's what she's already fallen into, if that party's any clue. That hollow shell of a celebration.

She wants to find love by giving up power. But she's giving up what she doesn't really have to get something they can't give. She's a master manipulator, that's how she's survived, but soon as she gives up any power, that tool just won't work.

Maybe she'll drop to a deeper sense of herself. She can't get there by climbing—she's already tried that.

It's risky, Mildred thought. And she didn't leave herself any toeholds. You're stuck in some black hole, alone, a stranger to yourself, a stranger to others. You're a little hard core of emptiness out of which something might—or might not—grow.

I know all this, Mildred told herself, but what's the point? It doesn't change anything. I can't tell her; she stopped listening to me a long time ago. And I let it happen.

I was my daughter's fool. She rose so much higher than I could imagine. My warnings were like a duck's squawks after the owl has grabbed her ducklings.

She ripped herself out at birth and has gone her own way ever since. Some chicks do that; they fight the shell all the way and come out pecking. Others just sort of nudge the shell open with their growing. Others practically die trying to get out.

At two years old she'd climb and swing, then stumble and fall on her own, deaf to my advice. Didn't I listen once in a while to Ma's words of wisdom? Why did I lose such faith in myself I let the gap between me and Bea grow, accepting her need to put me behind her? I knew she was ashamed of me. I cried out with clipped wings so she could fly to places I hadn't even dreamed about.

The silence between us grew and grew. Like the owl sometimes I feel like shrieking into that silence, howling until she finally listens to me. But it's too late now. What I know I have to hold within me like a hidden treasure. Like a miser I have to wait for her to find out for herself, the only way she ever understands anything.

What's the good of me knowing all this? If I were younger, I could be a teacher. But it took all my energy just to get through school—with all you have to put up with at my age: that teacher who resented me taking up space he said a young person should have, the students who think you're an old fuddy-duddy, the instructor who looked right through women over fifty. That was the shell I had to crack through.

One thing my secret knowing does; it sharpens the edges where I stand watching, thins the line between me and the children, between what I already know and what they'll soon discover. Trouble is, when they fall, deaf to my warnings, the ground breaks off beneath my feet too—and I fall with them.

It's like I'm still tied to them by a net. We're all tied together no matter how alone we each feel. So I can't just let her be. She's the seed of me.

Seed, root, shell, yoke—we're bound to the same cycle of life—and it doesn't do much good to ask a circle which end comes first.

All I know right now, she thought as she stood up slowly, knowing this moment of peace was over, *is I'm at the other, the far end of that circle.*

*   *   *   *

"Acting out: that's one thing I never got to do…No, I was the middle child, sort of quiet and lost, as they say…

"Well, believe it. My younger brother got to do the acting out. And then Millie—I really envied her when she'd hurl her soft-boiled egg against the linoleum in the midst of a tantrum…

"Yeah, she was my youngest. Being the mama, I couldn't join the fun, I got to clean up the mess.

"But now at my age, what's the risk? Most of my life I never spoke up, and where'd that get me? No one listens to me now, so why not speak up the best way I know—action…

"Yeah, you do—it's a lifesaver I can talk to you about all this. But the point is I don't care anymore how outrageous I am. I've got no money to lose, no reputation to uphold, little enough life left to live.

"Besides, it's exciting, fun, creative, dramatic, adds spice to the routine of watching my body come up with some new quirk, or fail to perform some ordinary chore. Watching yourself decay can be intense in the long run, but as a daily grind, it's dull as dishwater.

"Shucks, this was my big chance. Never had a debut…Now don't you laugh. Never had a proper swan song, never was a swan exactly…Yeah, never officially retired. If this is my second childhood, sure better seize the opportunity 'cause looks like there ain't gonna be a third…

"Ok, ok, I'm getting to it. But don't you see, the introduction's just as important as what happened…

"So Bea sails off, a sour lemon. I rattle around the house awhile, then settle into enjoying the luxury of it—space all to myself. Then, wouldn't you know it, along comes Dick and Jeanne and the three kids. They didn't just show up; they moved in. Claim radon gas—whatever that is—is leaking into their basement and could poison them if they stay there.

"No, I don't know how you get rid of it…

"Ok, ok, but after a week, it's obvious they're staying a whole lot longer than they said. Maybe even longer than the couple of months Bea's away. They claim they came to take care of me—the radon was just an excuse to do me good. Can you beat that? They're so busy taking care of me, they've taken over everything.

"Yesterday I ask Todd to get his dirty sneakers off the glass top coffee table. You know I'm not hung up on the amenities, but the dirt bothers me. Well, he just sneers at me and leaves his big feet right where they are. So I shove them off the table—not an easy feat, ha, ha—and he puts them back with a bang.

"'This is my house,' I tell him. 'Obey me here or go home.'

"Your house?" he snickers, "since when?" Now is that any way to talk to your great grandmother? It gets worse.

"Since before you were born." Of course, he's right, it's not my house, but I've lived in it longer than he's lived, period.

"Shut up, old bitch.' He doesn't even poke his head out of his comic book or whatever he's reading.

I could just smack him.

"Now Todd," Jeanne says oh so mildly, "don't be rude."

"Then she tries to smooth my ruffled feathers, but in her own way she's just as bad as Todd—stuffing Bea's favorite furniture in the garage, replacing it with pieces from her own home "for the time being." Antiques put out to mildew while we seek comfort (in vain) on stuff made to look at, not to sit on (sorta like Jeanne herself whose lap has as much appeal as a ski jump)...

"Now, Clare, you're the one who calls them Dick and Jane...

"Really! They're replacing our old faithful washer/dryer with a new one. I put my foot down. They're always buying the newest, the best; they've got to have everything. Their own house is stuffed full of appliances, gadgets, and enough supplies to keep them going through several nuclear disasters. They waste enough food to keep more than one soup kitchen in business...

"What do you think? Of course they ignored me. Why should I object to having something new? Why, I said, does something that works perfectly well have to be replaced?...

"Yeah, well one thing led to another. I went around turning off TV's in rooms where no one was watching and they blasted me for ruining their VCR taping. They're always busy taping programs they don't have time to see because they're busy watching other programs, each as stupid as the next. The microwave they brought in I managed to put out of commission accidentally, but with some satisfaction (I don't care what you say, those things radiate). When they left junk food all over the house, I crammed it into the garbage disposal, chanting 'Waste not, want not.'...

"Yeah, it does. You can see what I mean by fun and games. But of course they retaliated. No matter how much I grumbled, they let the kids run wild in the hallway outside my room at all hours of the day and night. And the last straw:

they hired a team of house painters to redo the kitchen. (Again, how could I possibly object to such a generous offer? I did object—but a fat lot of good it did.) This made a mess for weeks, while even more junk food detritus...

"Oh, you know—debris, garbage, junk—piled up in every corner. For all my years of not much to go on, I never lived in such squalor. Bea prides herself on creating this ordered, stable, tasteful environment—now it's turning into a parking lot at a shopping mall...

"Oh, you wouldn't believe it and she's going to have a fit—just what we all need. What really gets me is all the phoniness. Won't Bea be pleased to find her house 'fixed up' when she gets home? Isn't it grand to have a washer/dryer that doesn't creak? Aren't they such generous, friendly people? Except for Todd, who turns out to be rude to everyone, the rest of them are ultra polite. But never once in this whole time has any of them ever sat down with me at the kitchen table and had a real heart-to-heart. I'm just one more piece of old furniture they're eager to discard—or put their feet on.

"Wait a minute, Clare, someone's coming in. I better get off the phone...Yeah, I'll call you in a few days...Thanks a lot for listening to me go on and on. I don't know what I'd do without you...And good luck at the office— remember now, don't let them push you around, you've got the seniority. Bye."

✳   ✳   ✳   ✳

"Hi, Clare, it's me again. I can't talk very long—Barb'll be back from church soon. Sorry it's so early, it's the only chance I have for a decent conversation...Yeah, that's the news. I'm over here...Until Bea gets back, I guess. Must've overdone it on the acting out...

"Well, it got so all I wanted to do was shatter the phoniness. The day after I talked to you I locked the kids and their friends in the TV room and switched off the circuit breaker to that part of the house so I didn't have to listen to their hollering and shrieking any longer. At first without that steady electronic feeding, they almost went berserk. Then they got strangely quiet. By the time Jeanne called a locksmith to release them, she found them locked in every imaginable amorous position, like a scene from one of those porno books. She had to go to bed from the shock (sex doesn't seem to be her thing; she must channel all her lust into shopping).

"Then I got so sick and tired of cleaning up all their messes in the kitchen, I went the other way. I tossed eggs against the wall (in memory of Milly's antics), shot ketchup onto the ceiling, left trails of peanuts. I figured the parents would catch on and make the kids clean up after themselves, but I guessed wrong. You'd never figure it from their impeccable grooming, but Dick and Jeanne are really slobs themselves. So they hired a cleaning team to come in twice a week. More strangers in the house.

"I escalated my tactics. I took to complaining to visitors who called on the phone. I got on the extension and listed my grievances and demands, like a worker on strike...

"You bet. That was the last straw for Jeanne. She threatened to have me carted off to a nursing home if I didn't behave. "Obviously she has Alzheimers," she told everybody.

So I threatened to go live with Bruce and Barbara, figuring I could shame them into treating me with some respect. What about when Bea comes home and sees how mean they've been to me?...

"Yeah, I know, kids after her own heart, but still...

"So Dick said, 'Fine, go ahead.'"...

"Yeah, I know he's not your favorite, but you wouldn't believe what a sweet baby he was...

"Anyway, backed in that corner, I refused. They shipped me over here anyway. "Just for the time being." With the utmost politeness and concern. What hypocrisy—especially in the Dick department.

"Bruce and Barbara agreed, not so politely (I gathered that from overhearing the phone conversation)—they'd have me, but only if I brought no more than one suitcase and agreed to share a room with Lisa (I'm sure she's just tickled pink)...

"Lordy, Lordy, the price we pay for speaking our minds...

"Oh no, Clare, you don't have any extra room. It won't be so bad. I think I need a different tactic here though. Lay low. Being with Barbara and Bruce could be useful. It's like an instant replay of me and Art. Gives me a chance to observe, review my life, figure out why I put up with that nonsense for so long.

"It's already inspiring me to write. Listen to this: 'Car doors slam. Are you listening? Fists are clenched. Teeth are glistening...As we go along we pretend this is song...surviving in this Winter Wonderland.' I'll be a poet yet...

"Well, don't count on it. Try buying a lottery ticket instead...

"Now, don't you worry. I'll be fine. You've got enough on your mind. Soon Bea'll be back to restore order. Prying that family out of her place will be a challenge, even for a gal of her talents."

Are my edges melting—again? What makes me think each time I dissolve, it's gonna be the last time?

*   *   *   *

It's a flip of the coin: heads/tails, up/down. Or two sides of a mirror: inside/
out—set against each other but really two sides of a revolving door. Fame, blame,
it's all the same, rags or riches...Bigger is dangerous; smaller is scary. Others first/
others last—choose just one, backlash...Why's Bruce so sad? Used to sit in my
lap telling me stories, leaning back, listening to my stories. All sweetness then—
it's all gone now. Wish I could mirror him to himself—but I gotta cool it on the
"acting out—or it's off to goofeyville for me. No more trouble from me. What he
needs is a story about flying—steering straight into the wind, holding on, letting
the current and your own wings take you—a bird story, really—free of metal
shells.

Barbara? Wish I knew. The helpers need so much help. We've woven such a
glistening chain of helpers behind helpers backing up helpers, it's a wonder we
ever get on with our lives, even at such advanced—not to say "ripening"—stage
as mine.

Statues of Liberty, all of us—standing around stiffly searching for some new
object for our tender loving care—some new victim to save from our own systems, our crowns dropped around our necks like iron collars of duty. Such busy
little bodies, hungry as we feed the hollow, worker bees in the hive producing the
honey comb. "Want more stuffing?" instead of "Feed me." It's the female version
of the American Dream—filling up by filling others, rather than filling up and
spilling over. Note that with either system, others can get fed.

Trouble is—that moth beating her wings against the window—nothing she
does, no matter how hard she tries, will get her out into the air. She's got to find
another way out.

Clare helps Barbara help me help Bea help Corey help John help Bruce help
Dick help us help them help her help us. With all this help Bruce is just as beaten
down, abandoned, spoiled and neglected as he ever was.

What does any of this have to do with love? Isn't that the real issue here?

Just staying up late, staring into this fire after the girls have gone to bed, I wish
there was someone to talk to about all this. But as I say, who's listening? Clare's
spinning her own wheels. Bea's mapping out her own route to other sides of the
mountain. Guess she doesn't need any advice from me.

Like ashes in the fire, these words in my head, warming my brain.

✻   ✻   ✻   ✻

Squeals of delight? The children? I'm a mother again? Clare's voice is sing-ing—it's snowing outside! Am I glad? It's early October.

John's knocking at the door. Nobody's answering. I move to open it—I can't move. Am I dead?

No, I'm stuck in this bed—still asleep.

I curl out of the warm blankets and bundle up—a little round nuthatch. Not so cold out here after all, the sun's so bright. They're like kids—I feel like a kid too. Glad.

Flakes float down—huge wet flakes, huge wet sloppy flakes—leaves still sharp in their colors lit up in the rising light taking on a coat of white…chilled in their beauty, shocked in their colors—

John's knock—so insistent—why? Was something on fire? Something wrong? Why didn't somebody answer?

Amazing—so many snows, year after year, not one the same. I wonder if these crystals are a blessing or a warning. Winter's coming.

On Bea's hand a flake melts. A unique shape, they say. As different as you and me.

"Nothing lasts," she says.

"For which we can be both grateful and sorry." She looks up at me. A question she's afraid to ask is in her eyes. It scares me, but I look without flinching.

At least she can see—I can tell—the beauty of it. That's half the fun. Flip side, so to speak.

Me, I'm a colander—full of holes. My advice to her and Clare? Stop being pots and frying pans. Be holy by being holey—whole hog, whole-heartedly. Bring the outside in, the inside out. That way you're not locked in, you're not locked out.

Though eventually, for sure, you coast on out of here—down the drain, down the gullet, down the hatch. We all know that.

Did Clare really save me from a fate worse than death? Who knows? Maybe a nursing home wouldn't be so bad. Wouldn't put anybody out. God knows Dick can afford it. Trouble is, I don't want to miss the rest of what's going on around here. I don't want to be left out.

Gotta figure just which side of the threshold I'm on. Could I stand the luxury of it? Can they really afford it?—not just the money.

I'm glad to be here—out in the country, the woods near where I grew up. Here fixed sides seem silly—like comics in the Sunday paper—stiff, flat.

Can't bilocate yet. But maybe if I'd been there—at least in my dream—I could've opened that door for John. Where is he? Isn't he in San Francisco? Lord, I wish he'd move home—before an earthquake makes the whole state fall off into the sea.

God, look at how bent the trees are—heavy with the snow. Makes me shiver. Slippery too. Ok for them to be frolicking around—but I'm pretty brittle these days.

I can slide a little too. Everything's glistening. Sun at a slant and golden, like the leaves. Frost edging every leaf or half of leaf still in shade.

Bright white sharp against the orange and gold, brown and yellow leaves of fall. Dazzling. Bright blue—intense, multi flamed. When I stoop, I see a spider-web laced with drops, catching light, sending colors. It shifts and I see green, purple, blue again. Real magic, not pretend.

Shivering, Bea and Clare bundle me up—like an unwilling cocoon—and carry me into the fire. See what I mean? They're cold; I get wrapped. But I don't mind. Here, another kind of magic flames. The good-for-nothing bum in me stretches out.

I even tell them my dream. They figure it as memory.

"John's birthday next week," Bea says to herself.

"Wasn't he premature?" Clare obliges her remembering.

"Knocking to come in?" I wonder. They nod. Once again he's here too soon?

Never ceases to amaze me—this modern psychology. Womb/room; knocking/labor pains? Quite a brain here—maybe feeble but still alive and kicking.

*   *   *   *

This scene. Play it over. Play it forward. Play it backwards. Check out all sides. One more time.

Forward.

Bea's with John in the hospital room. A long time. Then Clare and I go in to see him. He's glad to see us, jokes about this excuse to come home. He doesn't look good. Hard to see the youngest, sweetest of the chicks shriveling up like this. Can't believe it's just pneumonia. Corey joins us.

A rush of wind—the rest of the family swarm in—Dick, Bruce, Barbara.

Bea's sitting on the bed with John.

"I wouldn't be doing that if I was you." Dick looks like the wrath of God.

"Doing what?" Her tone toward him is cool, cool, close to frigid.

"Cuddling a fag."

John glances at Corey; she shakes her head, puzzled.

A fag? We all gaze around, seeking confirmation yet avoiding each others' eyes. It makes sense that John's homosexual—but we'd probably just as soon not know.

Bea's obviously shocked. When she turns to John, he winces, sits up straight in the bed, stiff for her rejection. "Oh, dear" is all she says, but the tone is sympathetic.

No wonder Corey's so upset.

Now we're all surprised at Bea's response—where's the riot act? She takes John's hand. "Darling..."

"Not so darling if you get too close." Dick can't help taunting. Goaded by jealousy. "According to the doctor..."

John looks stunned. We all stare at Dick. "Hold it, big brother," John says quietly. "Please come here a second, I want to tell you something." His voice is thick, clogged with feeling.

Dick hesitates. He's obviously scared of something, but doesn't want his fear to show. He moves slowly toward John.

When he gets closer, John motions him to bend down so he can whisper something in his ear. Suddenly John grabs him around the shoulders and kisses him on the cheek. Dick pushes him away and pulls back horrified. "I don't want your dirty germs!"

John has fallen back into the pillows, too weak to move anything but a limp wrist, in an exaggeratedly fey gesture. "Aw, one little kiss won't hurt you, will it? Don't you remember that time in the shed when you and Stuart...?"

"Shut up!" Dick's face is pale, then splotchy.

We're amazed—a role reversal: John terrorizing Dick. But what's Dick so afraid of? Homosexuality isn't contagious. And he's hardly the type—not a sensitive or artistic bone in his body.

"Just keep away from me, you little faggot!"

"Burn, burn." John chants. "You lust after little boys—why not grown men? Burn, burn." He chokes, starts coughing.

"Just keep your dirty germs away from me." Dick sounds like he's fourteen.

John's beginning to sag. Corey leaps to his defense. "Why should we protect you?" she screams at Dick. "When did you ever protect us? The time you held me under water until I almost drowned? The time you shook the snake in our faces? The time you lured us up on the roof to see the bird's nest, then took away the ladder and tortured us until we begged for a way down? The time you locked John in the dark garage?" Corey's anger explodes through the cramped room. "I hope you suffer every bit of what you ever inflicted on us."

This is the point when someone needs to restore order, to say "Now children" in a firm tone and get all the planets revolving in their orbits again. I look to Bea for this. She knows her role and she knows when to use it.

But Bea is numb. Perhaps she's still reeling from the news about John being gay. Surely she isn't shocked by Dick's behavior.

So the frenzy goes on. Clare or me aren't about to step into Bea's shoes. I've done my time.

"You blaming me for his own polluted lifestyle?" Dick spits at Corey.

"I blame you for not caring, for turning him out of his own home—your own brother."

"Not caring? Who'd you think got him this room? I practically had to bribe the hospital to let him in."

Once the question of blame is raised, Bruce's guilt is pricked and he must enter the fray. "Why should we support his deviant behavior?"

"You afraid it'll call attention to your own deviant behavior?" challenges Clare.

"You kidding? I'm no fag."

"No, instead of pricks, you depend on sticks," Clare mutters.

"Are you nuts?!"

"You know—those needles of yours."

"What needles?" Barbara gasps. I can't believe she doesn't know.

"While you're so busy pinching pennies, he's out paying a fortune for coke."

"Coke?" Barbara looks both puzzled and stricken. She knows, at least I hope she does, Clare's not talking about coca-cola.

John coughs, one of those relentless, racking kinds of cough.

"Quick, call for help," cries Bea. John curls up away from her on the bed. She starts patting his back.

Corey rings for the nurse while saying, "She won't come."

"I'll get her," Clare rushes for the door, getting directions to the nurses' station from Corey.

In her panic to get help for John who does sound like he's choking to death, Clare leaves us—the family alone—trapped. Bea's stuck back somewhere. The only one who could save us is Clare, the outsider. No one else—not Corey, not me—is willing or able to come to the rescue. Now that Dick's and Bruce's worst selves are out in the open, they're free to bully the rest of us. We can't break out of the pattern; the pattern is breaking us.

There isn't a sound but John's coughing. Dick and Bruce sit there brooding like bad boys who've been found out, meanness building up in their faces. Barbara looks terrified, like she'd just as soon crawl under the bed and stay there until the storm blows over.

Bea's totally focused on John, feeling his forehead, soothing his back, keeping the blanket wrapped around him as he spasms. He tries to talk but his voice is so tight it sounds brittle.

Finally he stops coughing long enough to point to a book on the table next to his bed. He calls Corey over and scribbles something in the book. She nods.

"Watch out," Dick says to her without much enthusiasm. "You can catch his germs too."

She just glares at him.

"What's he want now?"

"None of your business."

"I asked her to call Scott," John gasps, then starts coughing again.

"Who's Scott?"

John can't answer. "His lover," Corey says, glancing at Bea.

"Oh no." Suddenly Bruce buzzes over and snatches the book from her. As Corey rushes after him, I see Dick, now sitting in a straight chair in the middle of the crowded room, stick out his foot to trip her. But she hops right over his foot and tackles Bruce's arm. Dick pulls back his foot real quick so no one will notice.

Bruce tosses the book to Barbara. She looks confused. "What's wrong with her calling him?"

"You want some faggot convention in your own home?"

"Oh, Bruce, don't be silly. He's your own brother."

"That doesn't mean we have to entertain every asshole—Gimme that!"

Barbara starts to hand the book to Corey. Bruce's hand grips her arm. I can just see the bruise forming.

Both Dick and Bruce are staring at Bea, as if daring her to do something about this. She just stares back, puzzled. My x-ray vision seems to see right into her—I watch her heart stop beating, then, by raw will, go on.

Where's that damn nurse? It sounds like John's lungs are turning inside out.

"Come off it," Dick shouts at John. "Stop being so dramatic."

Corey grabs the book and Bruce grabs her. "It's his life!" Barbara yells at him.

"You've got to be the ultimate victim," Dick's taunting John. "Always so hypersensitive."

Bruce wrenches the book out of Corey's grasp. He must be on crack; he's out of control. So's Dick. Don't ask me what his excuse is. "You're just overreacting!"

"Give her the book, god damn it," I shout. Startled, Bruce hesitates long enough for Corey to snatch the book.

"Call right away," Bea says.

Clare arrives with the nurse. The struggle over the book is suddenly mute. Another family secret: everyone fades into the background while the nurse attends to John.

And that's when it happens: I'm just sitting there minding my business when all of a sudden I start to see the whole thing again and again, from all sides.

I'm consumed with jealousy of my younger brother, Tommy, who never got punished—because he was the baby, because he was a boy. I watch him sleeping at night—so innocent, so unsuspecting—and imagine softly, gently, quietly smothering him to death with a pillow. I know how Dick must feel.

I'm burning up, poured into me my good spirits: the magic elixir, the best friend, the only one I trust, the one who has imprisoned me in this bottle—I'm the genie trapped in glass by a sorcerer I cannot see. In that liquid world, I sparkle, I soar, but when I'm poured out, I fizzle, then evaporate. I know how Bruce feels.

I tried to make a clean break of it, I tried to escape their sticky tendrils, but they've sucked me back into a world I no longer control, don't even understand. Why is Dick so mean? (Sure I felt jealous of Millie, but I didn't let that sour my love for her.) Why didn't John—or somebody—tell me he's gay? Why's Bruce acting so crazy? What's Clare talking about? Won't anyone please tell me what's going on here?

Bea, babe, I'm sorry I didn't tell you. I never figured you didn't know. But you shoulda given more sympathy to your own jealousy.

I'm not really a member of this family; I'm the stranger, the guest, the alien here, I have no right to say what I feel, I've got to try a little harder, give a little more than everybody else, I've got to keep my mouth shut and my shoulder to the wheel, and make sure what I think doesn't pop out somehow.

Yep, Clare, we kept our mouths shut together—until we finally broke and said our piece. Who says blood is thicker than water?

I'm standing up to Art, telling him to stop turning our kids into punching bags, asking him to act like a man. He leaves his mark on me, I won't let him take it out on the kids too. Barbara, Sweetie, the only way to take a stand is to turn your back and walk out on him. Stop supporting his weakness.

Corey, you know that. I don't know how you know, but you're not rushing into Bea's shoes—or are you? Can you change the pattern before it breaks you?

John, isn't it ironic? You're the last person I thought would be facing death with me. Suddenly we're the same age—one step away from that dividing line, that realm from which no traveler returns (as some poet puts it). Maybe you'll beat it, go on to ripeness. But if not, maybe we can hold hands and step into that darkness together.

Last but not least, Mildred: I see myself silent, too decayed to have a say; watching, cut off from, then plunged into everyone—swallowing my words, then speaking up; I see an old woman sitting here and feel my own vitality.

And then—still sitting in that chair, a stone in the angry stream, I'm all alone describing everything. No longer part of what I'm recording; all my energy goes to describing. I see patterns: how pretending you're not hurt makes you blame everybody; how envy's the other side of desire. I see these knots. I see how we're all tangled up together, yet moving on our separate paths like bugs in a row chewing on the same stick. Whether we sew and mend, or sow wild oats, or respond to every S.O.S., each of us a different thread, woven together without anybody able to choose the overall pattern.

It doesn't really matter—we're out of here too soon, however we go. Death happens to all of us eventually; birth's the only other thing that happens to us all. Between those two, we keep fighting the illusion of sameness, asserting how different we are, some rare bird pushing out of the common shell, forgetting the basics which are all the same: birth/death.

Alone I can be everybody; with them, I'm all alone.

But the point is we can turn it off and turn it on—just like my hearing aid. I can go into the silence of myself or into the sound of others. It's no one else who's operating that switch but me.

I've broken out of my shell, at last.

Thanks, folks, for cracking that egg.

*   *   *   *

Here comes my first poem:

> *America, honey, slow down.*
> *You're no IBM, you're no GrandAm, you're just human.*
> *Us beings, you know, grow slow.*
> *Don't just take my word: check this bean plant.*
> *Even though it did rush up when sprouting,*
> *it sat in that earth for an age, doing exactly nothing*

and after it sprung up, its leaves strolled out,
and its flowers dillydallied, dawdling with the ripening sun
trifling with the swelling moon
before they filled themselves up.

America, honey, slow down.
You deserve to take your own sweet time, and besides,
nothing's gonna happen any sooner anyway
just 'cause you're running around being so buzzing busy.

Aw, I guess this isn't really a poem. It doesn't even rhyme. But it's something that wasn't there before. It's something new. Something new I don't have to take care of all the time.

QUATRELOGUE

───────────── ▼ ─────────────

Is tragedy an obsolete form? A luxury for and about the high and mighty? Inappropriate for women? No longer relevant in a democracy?

According to one side of a dialogue composed by Carolyn Heilbrun and Catherine Stimpson, our theories of tragedy are masculinized.

> "Tragedy (despite extraordinary exceptions like Hamlet) rises like smoke out of the destructive gap between action and consciousness, between will and deep understanding of the consciousness of will...The tragic pattern for women, too often unrecognized, is the reverse. Tragedy, for many women characters, springs from the fact that consciousness must outpace the possibilities of action, the perception must pace within an iron cage...To oversimplify, the tragic man acts before he thinks; the tragic woman thinks and knows she cannot act." (*Feminist Literary Criticism: Explorations in Theory*, edited by Josephine Donovan, 68)

This position on tragedy is attributed to the Y point of view. Although literature is full of women characters without sufficient power over their own lives, propelled between marriage or suicide, contemporary life gives us many examples of women who are able to act before they think, not always tragically. The gate to the iron cage, while it still exists, has been cracked open. Our tragic hero, Bea, is one woman who has paced her way toward the American Dream, a SuperMom if not a Wonder Woman. And like Lear, reflection before action is not one of her strong points. She still believes she pulls the strings, that if things go wrong, she can make them right again. She knows, after all, how to learn from mistakes, profit from trial and error.

Heilbrun and Stimpson present another point of view on tragedy, one not so dependent on gender considerations. According to Viewpoint X,

"the sex of the tragic hero is…a matter of some indifference. Is it not the human pattern to conceive the illusion that we can control destiny, suffer for it until the will is lost and so become aware?…Will and action are masculinized, but will and action are human, and since all humans act necessarily from partial knowledge, there is a degree to which all persons must perceive will and action to be mistaken…because of the limitations inherent in being human. The tragic pattern is available to all…anyone who sees too late that perception must precede action…. Your ideal is male action made available to women, while for me the ideal is awareness, and the knowledge of the human price of action, however necessary it may be." (70)

A third perspective on tragedy is presented by Joseph Meeker's *The Comedy of Survival* which argues that the most appropriate form for our times is not tragedy but comedy. There's an inherent class bias in the structure of tragedy. No one assumes anymore that someone's exalted position in society automatically makes him a hero or that a fall from such status is tragic. People like to identify with the underdog and watch the top dog get his comeuppance; it's a form of entertainment for the masses to spy on the royals or listen to Washington or Hollywood gossip. It's not just *schadenfreunde* which makes us want to see folks brought down to earth. In a democracy, where the common woman or man is the hero, what counts most is not power or loss, but survival. Only the high and mighty can afford to wallow in failure. Heroic action—pushing to our limits—is commonplace for people who have to deal with poverty and discrimination on a daily basis. Comedy might be grounded in tragic events, but, according to the Wheel of Fortune, it demonstrates that what's been down so long is bound to turn up. And we're more likely to identify with and empathize with a protagonist who has had her share of scrapes and scratches.

As Susanne Langer puts it,
"Destiny in the guise of Fortune is the fabric of comedy…[It represents the protagonists's] triumph by wit, luck, personal power. Comedy is an image of human vitality holding its own in the world amid the surprises of unplanned coincidence." (*Feeling and Form*, 331)

Even people whose own actions bring them down, like Martha Stewart, are often scrappy enough to climb right back up again. Their lives are certainly not tragic. They are survivors. Sometimes survivors can also be heroes. The difference between a survivor and a hero is perhaps the clue to what might still be tragic in modern times. A survivor allies with self; a hero allies with and acts for the larger community in some way. When the hero cannot save the community or the community turns against the hero or the hero fails in integrity or courage to fulfill her commitment, the consequences can be tragic for hero and/or community.

A fourth perspective on the conventions of tragedy comes through systems theory. When the tragic flaw, although embodied in one person, represents the values of the whole system which indulges and feeds upon it, the tragedy affects the whole. The tragic hero acts for the whole family or institution or society, and everybody in some way pays the price. The tragic insight or epiphany is a lesson for everybody.

One modern form of tragedy is the consequence of industrial and technological arrogance and greed. The mechanization of natural life has alienated us from the organic process of birth, death, rebirth and turned us and parts of nature into replaceable parts/functions/roles. This is the tragedy the Romantic Poets tried to warn us about. Our life spirit cannot be relegated to new and used parts. Our physical lives and the lives of other species cannot be reduced to categories of matter. Such a materialistic, mechanical, fragmentary perspective has led, also, to splits between thinking and intuition, between principle and vision, which should work together like a pair of eyes. It has led, as well, to splits between sensation and feeling, resulting in all forms of disembodiment.

Dick, trapped within power and privilege, suffers from thinking split from intuition; he's separated from any real connection with others, obsessed with finding the sexual glue of intimacy, unable to see the whole. Bruce, the victim, the reluctant soldier, trying to self-medicate with drugs, suffers from feeling split from sensation; he wants desperately to find a way back into connection, but is locked out by his own locked up feelings. Bea's tragedy is the loss of John, the only person besides Corey who could have guided her into a new life.

Within a healthy system, connection and consciousness converge; in this novel they are split apart. The whole is wounded. All must connect, all must be aware if the whole is to be healthy, productive, life-affirming. Otherwise, the waste of human potential, the restrictions on people's growth through abuse, neglect, homophobia and other forms of discrimination, exploitation—all this is tragic.

An America which has lost its founding democratic ideals of freedom, justice, equality, which invades other countries, exploits foreign peoples, destroys its own matrix, neglects and discriminates against its own people, is a tragic America, using its own rhetoric to justify hypocrisy. An institution founded to foster progressive values which mistrusts and degrades its employees and clients is a tragic institution. A dysfunctional family which neglects and abuses any one of its own members is a tragic family. Context within nested context—abused children growing up to become passive or malicious citizens—the whole web of connections can be shattered by the failure of any one dimension.

PART FOUR: THE HUM

BEA'S TRANSFORMATION

Everything's fallen apart. Like after a big windstorm or earth shaking—rubble, ruin. This time I can't put the pieces back together, like I did after Jack died—put the puzzle together again even though one piece is missing. This time it's all shattered.

They want me to weave it again, like a spider. What they don't get is that I'm not the spider, I'm caught in the web just like everybody else. Spiders sit outside their webs; flies are caught inside. Only the spider can move through her own web without sticking to it. How quickly she wraps her prey into that silk shroud which looks so much like a cocoon.

One touch of that web and we're all spinning and reeling. I'm just like everybody else, struggling to fly free.

Poor Bruce, on the phone just now—apologizing, apologizing. For what? For being mean to his brother? So what else is new? How was he to know how sick he—? How were any of us to know? Who ever heard of such a thing? Anyway, it's not my place to forgive him. I'm just sorry he feels so bad.

Soon Dick will be here for this meeting about the business. Now that he's blown it, he wants me back in command to take the flak for him. But that's the least of his problems. The tighter he gets, the harder it is to touch him—and the more he needs just that. What would help him? A new wife? Some friends? Someone who doesn't expect him to be all he's set himself up to be.

Suddenly they're clamoring for things as they were. They want me back at the center of things shielding them from their failures, protecting them from responsibility, buffering their successes, cushioning them from blame, soothing the sting of their guilt.

And Corey last night, so eager to share her school preparation with me. But I'm not a teacher anymore. I was interested in the dragonfly pictures—fascinating how they crawl right out of their split skin—but I didn't want to help her figure out how to teach the class. She's sorta like that nymph herself, crawling into womanhood without much help from us. Even though I judged her for not being as outgoing and powerful as I am, was, I must've been afraid she'd become too much like me. Daughters do. I never let her be a princess because I didn't want her to become a Queen. Queen Bea—huh! And I didn't want to do to her what Mama did to me, make me the little mother before I had time to grow up on my own.

And John, where are you now? Maybe it's time for you to come home, honey, before that city crashes down around your ears. It's only a matter of time before a big earthquake.

I just hope Clare isn't expecting me to restore order too. She can do it herself if the spirit moves her. She was my real partner, she's got what it takes if anyone has. But the old order's gone. It should've been destroyed.

The old order left him out. My baby, an outsider—scorned, made fun of, isolated, scapegoated. How could we let that happen?

Each struggle, each touch makes every other part of the web quiver.

Only Mildred doesn't seem to mind the shreds we're left with. She's not mending anything and she doesn't seem to expect me to. The way she keeps teasing me, calling me "Little Miss Take Charge," I know she's warning me—not to try to fold my wings and curl back into that cramped and brittle shell of who I was. Of course she never minded the raggedyness as much as I did—and now threadbare, she's almost transparent.

But who am I now? They want me to be who I was—and I can't let them know who I am, because I don't know.

Oh god, I wish I could cry. Tears spring up, then dry up. I feel like an empty well. Maybe if I could get out of this city and back to the waterfall. Maybe I'm not dried up, but dammed up.

I just keep seeing their faces. Their faces—remorseful, desperate, eager, loving, waiting, blaming, praising—keep pressing into me. And it feels like my heart is pushing back, crying out for room to breathe. I gave them life—isn't that enough?

Who is there to take care of me, to comfort me, to listen, to forgive?

I hear a humming. Into the cave of my chest, into that hollow. John's voice?

Poor Barbara, she was so desperate to help us. Her skin's taut like old rubber, a ball that's been kicked around too much.

The baby raccoon crying all night. I heard her song, but I didn't—couldn't help her.

My baby sister crying all night. I was trapped in a crib. I knew that crying does no good.

John, you were playing a whole new music. And I didn't even stay to listen. And when I could finally hear it, it was too late.

Darling, please give me another chance. Please play again. I can almost hear that song—outside, down the street, on the radio. Each touch sounds a note, each string weaves a song in the web.

Maybe I can sing it. It's pressing up into my chest.

Why is my heart closing, shutting up like a dried pod?

It pauses, watches everything—the fixed photo—sees clearly how it all fits together, with or without me—and doesn't care anymore whether they understand me, whether I understand them. It really doesn't matter.

What matters is how it fills with the music, how the aching eases away as it swells with notes, chords, keys merging into soft harmonies
pounds with a new rhythm
and explodes
and I'm riding like an overflowing bucket out of this well,
beating my wings against dark, damp rock walls
I'm rising out of this shell of broken dreams, bruised egos,
sudden changes, last chances, worn gifts, like a startled bird
into a place where no one waits
and no one arrives
not even me.

"When Bumblebees in solemn flight
Have passed beyond the Sun—"
—Emily Dickinson

FAMILY CHORUS

Mildred: Old age is something we could have in common. Even if I'm not there to share it with her, she would know how I suffered with my arthritis, how feeling pulses through us even when our arteries are clogged, how some memories are bleached out by the present moment and others sharper in focus...all that I never shared with her because she was too busy or too worried or too caught up in the tangle of her life to notice. And probably wouldn't have understood anyway, not until she felt it herself...which she would if she grows old...

"Poor mother," she would say when the weariness sets in, "how did she stay spry so long?" Or "Now I know how she felt when she couldn't go swimming any more." Or "I understand now what she meant when she said that old age ain't for the faint of heart."

Corey: The ambulance gets to the apartment building just as I do. Behind the stretcher, I can't believe the men are rushing to Mom—sprawled out on the floor in front of the couch. When mouth-to-mouth resuscitation doesn't seem to work, one of them rips through her sweater and blouse down to her slip and then just cuts through that and her bra too—and starts pounding on her chest.

Pounding on a door that will not open.

"Hey ho, nobody home."

Bruce: The C.O. caught it in the chest. The private got it in his privates. All I lost was a finger. How lucky can a guy get?

One month in, one month out, from muddy bunker to clean sheets, firefights to firesides, mine sweeps to vacuum cleaners—how lucky can a guy get?

Dick: What can you do when the system breaks down? When bandits seize control of the driver's seat?

It's like a terrorist takeover, a worker's strike, a guerilla war—sane men can only sit back and hope for order to be restored by the proper authorities, with maximum efficiency and minimum force. We don't want to be reduced to their level of desperate, barbaric action, but we just can't tolerate this kind of disruption. It means death to all we hold dear.

Clare: Oh god, how she'd hate this. She's hooked up to machines that pump her blood, push breath in and out of her lungs, keep her heart alive. I wish I could give some of my life. Her hand's soft and warm, but she isn't here.

When does life leave a tree? We used to wonder about this in the woods. There're so many stages of life and death—the seed sprouting, the crumbling log. Once a tree's chopped down, it can't grow, blossom, shed leaves, sway in the wind, receive nests, shelter birds.

Her hand's like a shell, an empty seed pod. In this darkness I can replay our life together: the security she gave me, creating the business together, the losses, the calm after the storm, and love growing in that empty place.

Mildred: Old age we could've had in common. Everything else in her life was different: the rich and devoted husband, the career, the business, the having it all, the successful children (even the ones she judged unsuccessful). Of all my kids she is the one who knew her way around: how she spoke, hobnobbed with the rich and famous, spent her money...we had nothing in common once she passed her childhood, which was quicker than most.

But success must be a greater trap than failure. Like a tight suit you expand to fit, you fill it too fully and can't slip out of it as easily as the baggy suit of failure.

Corey: My dream haunts me. "How would you like it if somebody took away your clothes?" I was so mean to her.

A slight pulse, that's all they could find. Oh, her face, so grey. Otherwise, no movement. I can't believe she's so still. Can a failed heart return? Can it bring back the rest of her?

At least it keeps beating—hoping, maybe, to mend the wounds, pull it all back together, feed the separate parts.

How would you like it if somebody took away your shelter, your clothes, the shell of your life? Here in my body, my clothes, my shelter I feel like crying out to her: Now that you know what it's like, come back, come back. Don't reject us twice. We miss you.

Bruce: I didn't want to go. They drafted me. Not bright enough to be a pilot but sturdy enough to be a foot soldier. Dick wanted to go. They wouldn't let him. Said his glasses were too thick. I was in perfect health. (What's a stutter between enemies?) Me, the wimp. While Dick played football, I played Chinese Checkers. Compulsively. I could beat every preppie around. So what? What I liked about Chinese Checkers is that you could jump guys without wiping them out.

What a joke. Those gooks didn't just wipe guys out; they cut them open, chopped their heads off, stuck their privates in their teeth. When our patrol saw that, we split—and I mean quick.

Dick: Mom's heart, they say, is healthy enough, but it's rebelled; won't respond to orders from her head. And without that connection, that higher intelligence, it can't survive for long. All we can do is hook it up to these life support machines until it decides to listen to its own brain again.

When the economy breaks down, you have to tighten up the monetary flow, to bring the system under control again. Unfortunately business lags behind medicine that way; we don't have such efficient machines to plug everything into when the market collapses, panic sets in, and prices rise off the charts. No financial emergency room procedures operate as reliably as these marvelous inventions.

I hope they work.

Clare: Dear God, please let the music come back. She started with such lively music; at the end she found real harmonies. None of these machines—for all their beeping and buzzing—can make that kind of music. Not even our computers could sing those melodies.

Her body's a deserted ruin. But I feel she's still close by. Silent for a change, very, very silent.

Please, Bea, if you can't speak to me, at least hum. Nothing.

Mildred: Old age would make us even at last. That's when differences shrivel up. A final polishing to bring out the best in us. Some grow worse with age, of course, but I bet she'd glow like dried grasses in the sun. And we'd have glowed together, even though I'd be long gone.

But she didn't hold on for the long haul, she skipped out too soon. Her heart betrayed her, failed the marathon. She'll miss the best, the harvest, when you can let go of all the striving and doing and just enjoy being here. And I'm left for the last lap, to go it alone. Still, she crossed the line before me.

"Weeping willow, weeping willow, weeping willow, wait for me. Any moment, any moment, any moment, I'll join thee."

Corey: It's the first time I ever brushed her hair. My first chance to mother her. But of course she can't respond.

If only I could have cradled her, comforted her: Mother to her baby.

But her heart was just too heavy, too tough. Like it set off its own avalanche, fell through the ice, dropped to the bottom—and no one can retrieve it.

Soon we'll have to disconnect her...dress her in her gold and blue dress...bury her body.

But not cheerfully. No, not at all cheerfully.

She used to try to cheer me up when I was down. Stop complaining. Stop moping around. If you have to do something, she'd say, you might as well do it cheerfully.

But this time there's no way I'm gonna cheer up.

Bruce: Firebase Charley. They dropped you in, they pulled you out. In and out of the great dragon's belly. First time I ever smoked. Stoned for a month. Imagined gooks and geeks behind every bush. Never really saw the V.C. alive and in person—only the bodies.

My finger just dangled there after the explosion. I was so surprised. detached. Amazed it still held on by such a shred of flesh. Just stood there watching it. That's when Al grabbed me, pushed me down into the mud as another shell exploded. The pain finally jabbed into my brain. That's when I screamed.

The C.O. has caught it in the chest. The private took it in his privates. All I lost is a finger. How lucky can a guy get? No use crying over spilt milk.

Dick: What more can we do? We have to trust the miracles of modern medicine, I guess. We've done all we humanly can to bring her through. Now we'll just have to wait for her economy to bounce back, her system to restore itself, her heart to bow to its ruler.

Was it all my fault?

Clare: "Brain dead," they say, a "vegetable." Even picked vegetables can ripen; but her body can't. When her heart stopped, the brain, starved for blood, died.

She can't die in peace. She's strung up by wires and cords to machines which force life—or what seems like life—into her body. This technology allows the family to do its thing, unchanged despite all that's happened. If conflict is life, the family is still alive—but not well.

Guilt, manipulation, denial, blame. Everyone disagreeing what to do? And this is nothing new, I'm gonna have to make the final decision. They just go round and round, lashing out, backbiting, growling like a pack of starving dogs. The bills pile up, the hospital is pressuring us to decide. She made it clear she didn't want to be kept alive.

Your spirit's hanging in the background, waiting for some release. We've got to let you go.

I'm sorry. Forgive me. Bless us.

"An aged Bee addressed us—
And then we knelt in prayer—
We trust that she was willing—
We ask that we may be.
Summer...Sister...Seraph!
Let us go with thee!
In the name of the Bee...—
—Amen!"
—Emily Dickinson

MENDING

Mildred First:

Clare's still grieving, watching the sun go down like it's some ritual for Bea. "This is it—the moment."

"Past the moment," I can't help muttering.

"No, look—it's just setting into those trees."

"That's an optical illusion. The sun's already set." She's glaring at me. She gets my point but she seems to resent it.

How can I distract her from all this grief? Let's get on with it. "Look at the drop falling from the paddle. When does the moment end—when the drop hits the water or when the circle it makes dissolves?"

She isn't buying it. "You're getting too philosophical for me." The boat drifts as we watch the sunbeams clutch at the raggedy tips of the hemlocks, then slide from view.

"My last sunset," I can't help announcing. Such a chill just as soon as the sun goes. Good thing I've got two blankets. And I'm still feeling sorry for myself.

"Nonsense." I can tell Clare isn't really listening.

"Last night I dreamt I went to get my hair done and when I looked in the mirror, it wasn't white or even grey, it was brown again—and no wrinkles either."

"Wish you were young again, I guess. Time for you to go in now. It's getting cold."

Which means she must be getting cold—makes sense since I have all the blankets. "No, I want to see the colors. Here, take this." Well, what'd you know—she's actually accepting one of my blankets.

Often as I've heard it, the heron's squawk still surprises me.

"It's her, her spirit, I know it is." Clare's not usually so intense with her feelings. Does it make her feel better to watch the huge bird rise and curve above us? Yes, those wide, wide wings could be Bea's.

No more stalling on my part—she's rowing us back to shore. I hope she goes slow enough for me to lose myself in the fading light, float away like the heron into the clouds, entranced by the colors. What are these tears rolling down my cheeks—ecstasy or grief? I still feel so empty when Clare refers to Bea. Is my numbness anger? "Careful now, Clare."

I needn't worry. Between Clare's skill and Corey's pulling the boat in from the dock, we land without a hitch.

The three of us sitting here on the dock is almost an evening routine. We've stopped arguing about Bea's life—whether she made bad choices and had to bear the consequences, whether she was a victim of fate, whether anything we could have done would've saved her, whether she died too soon.

The milkweed pods have opened. That's how I want to go—like one of those feathered seeds, drifting softly on the breeze, settling gently someplace new. Nothing spectacular. And not before the time is ripe.

I see, I hear all this, but I just can't write any of it down. I figured I'd finally broken out of the pod, but I am the pod. I thought I'd become a poet, but my words scatter across the paper.

> *"Some things that fly there be—*
> *Birds...Hours...the Bumblebee—*
> *Of these no Elegy...*
> *How still the Riddle lies!"*
> —Emily Dickinson

Corey Last

Funny how my biggest thoughts come this time of night when we're huddled around the wood stove, gazing at the glow. Like staring into a night sky.

Did the blue nova explode? Implode? They thought only red stars died, they were sure this was a flaw, but it wasn't. It died 170,000 years ago and took that many light years for us to see it—the first dying star to be seen by the naked eye in 383 years. A thousand years before it died, it fused. It was an adventurer, not like our sun which will probably bloat into a red giant and then shrink into a white dwarf. A supernova—it ran out of energy.

What's that Clare's singing? "Farther along we'll know all about it. Farther along we'll understand why." Funny how sweet her singing voice can be, without that trace of bitterness you can hear when she speaks.

"Whata you thinking about, Clare?" Oops, did I wake Mildred?

"About a singing tree in our woods back home."

Mildred's perking up. "A bee tree! We had one too—huge and full of bees."

"Full of honey too."

"Can't go too close or what you'll get is swarming and stinging. Bees don't take kindly to someone messing with their singing."

"The hum's so loud it sounds like the tree's going to rise up and take off."

"I wish we had one around here. And what you been thinking about, Gram?"

"Bea—been reading her journal. Seems she knew she was just Queen for a Day—any woman who thinks different's a real fool."

But I'm tired of talking about Mom. Instead I'm thinking about John. I wonder what dying is like. And whether he will be reborn again. In my lifetime? Will I know him?

I hear his voice saying to me, "It's real challenging, Corey. It's like turning a somersault."

John was good at somersaults. I can see him now, twisting his little head under, without even bracing himself with his arms, and flipping over. I was good at cartwheels. Even Mom said so.

> *"It's all I have to bring today—*
> *This, and my heart beside…—*
> *Be sure you count—should I forget…*
> *This, and my heart, and all the Bees*
> *Which in the Clover dwell."*
> —Emily Dickinson

EPILOGUE

▼

Although tragic heroes tend to be more powerful or charismatic than any of us, the irony of tragic insight is how we (and, hopefully, they) discover they are, in fact, no better than the rest of us. Their limitations are what we all encounter as we mature and age: the loss of ideals, disappointments of romance, lack of perfection, failures of friendship, exposures of secret vulnerabilities, constrictions of power, frailties of our bodies. Tragic redemption for them comes when they realize this through an epiphany, as Bea does when she moves from control and bitterness to forgiveness and empathy. Tragic redemption comes for us vicariously to the extent that we can identity with them, experiencing the catharsis of suffering with them. Experiencing glee in the face of another's downfall not only prevents our own redemption, it attaches us to that suffering. The tragic epiphany ultimately is one of empathy or compassion: the compassion the hero feels for other characters and the empathy we, the audience, feel for the hero.

To what extent does Bea's transformation involve a loss of ego, in the Buddhist sense? As women become more explicitly powerful, our awareness of ego needs as well as ego abuses is becoming more apparent. We are vulnerable to the same hubris in which many men are practiced. This may not be a stage we can avoid. Familiar as many women have been with an egoless state (self sacrifice in the most martyred sense), one cannot be said to have transcended ego when one never developed much of an ego in the first place. The fuller spiritual growth associated with the "death of the ego" cannot be confused with the holiness projected upon some women by a patriarchal society which cannot itself reach or even truly believe in that ideal.

Ego or no, the spiritual insight aging women might realize through a renunciation of power and possessions is probably somewhat different from a man's. Most women are born knowing we are not the center of the universe, that we are intimately connected with others, that receptivity and love are necessary to survival. Paradoxically, Jungian psychology suggests that we move closer to the opposite gender as we age, men finding wholeness by integrating their more feminine side, becoming more receptive, tuned to others, reflective—while women move closer to the male experience, becoming more assertive, more public, more goal oriented. A Superwoman like Bea, who has mastered both family and career, should be a balance of masculine and feminine, but in fact "successful" women like Bea know how to operate in a patriarchal system, juggling male-identification while keeping a polish on their feminine personas.

This issue of ego or self has become an interesting contested ground as East has met West in the last few decades: Buddhist teachings clashing with western psychology over the importance and fluidity of self. A major goal in most western psychological theories—the development of a healthy ego and resilient self-esteem—is a lesser stage, perhaps even a hindrance, for Buddhists. Hinduism, as also imported, talks about the large Self, with a capital S, and the small self, with a lower case letter, suggesting an inclusive compromise between self-development and self-transcendence.

Whether ego is the apex or simply a rudimentary step, I like the perspective offered in an interview with Maxine Hong Kingston whose work integrates the best of both East and West:

> "I think we always have an identity. I think we're born with identities, but we're not aware of it. That's all. For some people, there comes a time when they're aware of it, and then they can tinker with it or try to grow it better, or they can grow up. But it seems to me we always have one, and I don't think I understand that about letting go of ego…In a sense of being a show-off and selfish—that kind of ego—I feel a struggle with that, with trying to be less selfish…I think of ego like that, which I don't think is the Buddhist sense of ego. I think in the Buddhist sense, proper selfhood involves the sense that all living beings are connected. I can feel this ring of connection, or I can see it as an electric grid in which we're all connected to it and we are all life. I guess that is what "no self" is. It's just—all of us."
> (p. 64, *Shambhala Sun*, January, 2005)

From a systems point of view, this "no self" or capital Self is the whole system. Just as the ego may play an important role in that whole, a strong centering function perhaps, its dominance can be detrimental to the whole, whether that whole is a single individual, a family, or a larger institution. In a feudal system, the ego is king; in a capitalist system, the ego is the capitalist or the corporation; in a patriarchal system the ego is male. As Virginia Woolf put it, the woman's role in a patriarchal system is to mirror the man's image at twice its natural size. In a family, the ego can be either parent or child.

In our contemporary mass society, we honor and reward narcissism in performers and public figures more than we do service because they carry that ego need for the whole anonymous mass of us. In the global context of mass media and overpopulation, what most people lack are not opportunities for service but opportunities to be noticed, to capture the attention of others. Rather than making this need part of a natural exchange and communication whereby I pay attention to you and you pay attention to me, this repressed need becomes a secret currency of celebrity projected onto a famous few.

Tragically the needs of the whole system are neglected when so much energy goes to prop up the ego dimension. Service to all goes unrecognized and unrewarded while self-aggrandizement is lionized. The family's dependence on Bea's success blinded them to her vulnerabilities; her compulsion toward inflation made her deaf to the needs and contributions of others. It was only when she inadvertently stepped out of this system that it collapsed, allowing her access to a transformation otherwise remote to someone in her position.

When we compare the human form of transformation to other natural forms, ours is not very dramatic. Most of the amazing changes happen within the womb, as we transition from worms to amphibians to animals to humans, all these changes wrapped up within our brains. Out of the womb we move in fairly simple progressions, without drastically changing form, from small to large then shrinking again—expansion, then contraction. Without cocoons, carapaces, shells or skins to shed, we have to be content with internal transformations.

But the lesson is the same, whatever its shape. Attachment to any one form or any one stage of that form can be fatal. Whatever our identity (ego or not) and role in a larger system, we know that we can't just transcend that structure; we must allow our position to change at its own pace. If we don't trust that process, the next generation might have to, just to survive. The world that Corey and John are negotiating is not the same world Bea set out to conquer.

It's sad but not tragic that Bea did not survive her own transformation. As Karen Armstrong points out,

> "Enlightenment [is] the discovery of a sacred realm of peace in the depths of one's own self and thus the finding of strength to live creatively in this world

of pain and sorrow...Compassion is the key to religion, the key to spirituality. It is the litmus test...in all the major world religions...When you dethrone yourself from the center of your world and put another there, you achieve extasis, you go beyond yourself..."
(p. 39, *Shambhala Sun*, January, 2005)

Tragic insight, therefore, is not merely about loss or failure; it's about pushing the limits so that we can grow beyond our selves into deeper, wider unities.

PART FIVE: THE HONEY

"Humming the quaintest lullaby
That ever rocked a child...

...The Bumble bees will wake them
When April woods are red."

—Emily Dickinson

COREY'S JOURNAL

February:

I don't know. I've been searching in every nook and cranny of the past and I can't find what Marion wants me to find. We weren't a between-the-lines type of family. It was all out there in blatant color.

Anyway, I'm just going to stick with this bee lore stuff. It's what I know how to do: research.

(*The Queen is dead. Long live the Queen?* No, no, no. I reject that script.)

March:

Marion really seems hung up on John, I guess because of being gay herself. She says the first cases of AIDS were diagnosed in 1981. I explained what a backwater of hypocrisy and respectability we lived in, but I'm not sure what difference it would have made if we had known. I knew there was some kind of gay "cancer" going around, but I didn't know John was gay—I mean, he hadn't actually told me before he was sick so I didn't make a connection, I guess because I didn't want to think he was that sick.

She told me a story about a friend of hers who died of AIDS. When he knew how sick he was, he wanted to go home one last time—for his birthday. When he called his mother to ask if he could come home, she responded, "How can you do this to me?" She quickly handed the phone over to his father who said, "How can you do this to your mother?" He never went home; he died on his birthday. At least Mom wasn't that bad.

Marion said how sad it was John never came out to us, except at the end, that he couldn't share Scott with us until it was too late. I asked her if she'd come out to her family and she said yes, but sadly. "It didn't make that much difference, except to my own peace of mind. They don't understand. They love me in spite of it."

We talked about the tragedy of dying young, of the young men who were killed in the invasion of Panama, the flag-draped coffins on TV. So many more young men are dying of AIDS, without the trappings of heroes.

"War doesn't seem a more noble cause than sex," Marion said. "Both can be useful for liberation; both can cause untold damage."

Then she really caught me off guard.

She asked me to tell her about Bea's retirement party. Although I had mentioned it in my story, she still didn't have a clear idea what actually happened.

"Whatdaya mean, what happened? She stepped down from her throne, that's what happened?" If I could feel my resistance, you can bet she did too.

"Describe it for me."

"Describe what?"

"The whole scene."

The whole scene was burned into my memory like some late night movie I've watched over and over. And that's how I described it to her, like some old movie.

"Ok. Well, of course, there was Bea, resplendent in gold and blue, gliding past her bevy of fans, pecking cheeks, squeezing shoulders, whispering, making us laugh. Her aura of charm at full tide, she sailed through the crowd with the charisma of a queen." Once I got into it, I started sailing myself.

"The party was well orchestrated—nothing left to chance. Grandchildren rigid in starched suits and ties, frilly dresses. Dutiful sons and daughters-in-law rehearsing speeches.

"It was quite a feast—sit down dinner for over two hundred people, surf and turf with all the trimmings, no expense spared.

"After dinner, Big Brother Dick tapped his champagne glass with a knife. His speech went something like this:

"'Mother, tonight we pay tribute to you, an exceptional woman. You've done what many men couldn't do, and more. You've created a highly successful business, Harmony Enterprises, integrating the highly technical world of computers with the all-too-human process of teaching, as you have also integrated the highly competitive world of finance with the all-too-ethereal world of music. You have brought to this venture all your skills of invention, of organization, of dealing with people, of shrewdness and of perseverance...'" And so on. Blah, blah, blah."

"Excuse me," Marion interrupted, "but what exactly was Bea's business. I never quite figured it out. Did she invent something?"

"Well, sort of—she was one of the first people to imagine a computer recording music as it was played—so that people could actually compose by improvisation. She connected the keyboard of a computer with the keyboard of a piano and then took it from there. Everyone was skeptical at first because music is so much more complex than computers—but these days, of course, the technology is taken for granted. Her forte was applying all this to education—developing programs for teaching kids about music in a creative way so that they wouldn't be just listeners but players and potential composers too."

"Impressive."

"Yeah. Anyway, then it was Bruce's turn. His speech went more or less like this: "'When I think back on all you've accomplished, I recall the excitement we felt at your enthusiasm—how you had that old piano in the garage wired to that old computer and kept sending us back to the bench to play, even though we couldn't hear what we were playing because it was all being translated into beeps and letters."

Just about everyone there, except those of us familiar with Bruce's passive aggression, seemed charmed.

"Of course like the Wright Brothers you hadn't yet perfected the Music Maker we know today where kids can hear what they're playing, but Mom, I want you to know what willing guinea pigs we were. I loved every moment of our growing up with your searching, your brilliance, your sense of adventure. I only hope I can pass some of your spirit on to my own children.'"

"Then it was John's turn."

"Aren't you the third child?" Marion asked.

"Yeah, but I'm a girl."

"That's not fair."

"When you're lining up to go to hell, who wants to be first? Anyway, Dick skipped me. John stood, raised his glass, and said something like, "Mom, I love you." Then he pulled out a musical instrument and played a song, one of those new age songs. You would've liked it. Kinda spacey. It was sweet.

"Applause was scattered. I looked over at John protectively and he crossed his eyes. It took me by surprise and I started to giggle. Then John started giggling and it was like being kids again. We couldn't stop.

"Suddenly Mom's voice roared through the room: "Leave it to John—" Her scorn was blatant—and almost surprising. (John, after all, was her favorite.)

"And then—just in time to clean up this mess—it was my turn. Loudly Dick called on me. But I was pissed at her for embarrassing John, so I didn't say anything."

"'Well?' Dick asked, resuming his duties as master of ceremonies.

Well, nothing, was my response.

"Again the Queen's roar: "Look at these kids. Dick's worth at least $100,000 a year; Bruce's worth $50,000 and little John's worth nothing." I wasn't even worth mentioning. Good thing I didn't say anything—she would've been in her glory mocking me too.

"But that wasn't all. Then she went on one of her rampages. Interrupted the next tribute with a speech of her own: 'Lest I have the kind of kids who sit around waiting for me to die so they can have their inheritance, let me announce now that I intend to divide my share of the company's assets, my 80%, among my children, NOW. This will make you four very rich indeed. But it will also require the utmost responsibility.'

"We kids looked like somebody who'd just won the lottery without even playing. But I could see strings closing around those piles of green bills.

Besides, this was just a premature revelation of her will, which was pretty much the same as it had been all along, with provisions for Mildred and Clare and others too. It didn't mean much in any case because, although she had plenty to live on, even after Dick jumped the gun, she never had a whole lot of control over her money—it was mostly tied up in investments and red tape. We all continued to have the same incomes we always did—Clare wasn't actually fired, Mildred was supported by company pension funds, we kids had jobs, we were all a long way from unemployment or welfare or poverty—and a long way from winning the sweepstakes too. Typical ploy though—Did she want to see us fighting like dogs over that imaginary bone? Deprivation is relative, but it takes many forms.

"Then, out of the blue, John picked up one of the famous Music Makers and started playing music with international rhythms: Greek, Nigerian, Peruvian. That was my clue to dance. I couldn't believe he was going ahead with this—our gift to her—in the face of her fury. But I couldn't let him down, so I danced.

"Smack dab in the middle of our performance, the Queen walked out—followed by her entourage."

"Ykkes."

"Yeah, sometimes she could be a monster without half trying. But that was years ago. Everything's changed since."

"You still sound pissed."

"Aw, what's the point of anger now?"

"Claiming it, having a right to it, releasing it."

"Nyeh." How would I ever sort it out? Was I more angry at her for leaving us or for never being quite there for us? Aw shit, she did her best. Her best just wasn't good enough. Was that her fault?

"You could write her a letter just saying some of what you're feeling now."

"She'd never have time to read it."

"Maybe not, but wouldn't it feel good to say it?"

"Good?" I laughed. "No, it would feel *bad*."

Marion smiled. "Sometimes nothing feels so good as being bad."

Suddenly in my peripheral vision I had a glimpse of Mom walking out the door and in my mind's eye I raced after her, screaming for her to stop, I had something to tell her, but she wouldn't, she kept marching out as if she hadn't heard me, so I took a flying tackle and hit her right behind her knees, knocking her heels off

and then I fell into a pit, dark, deep and slimy, with muddy sides and no light above and I began to sob and sob as if I would never stop, as if that's what my body had been designed for, endless sobbing, and it had finally come into its own.

When I came to, I could feel soft fingers on my forearm and I looked up into the kindest face in the world—Marion's. She didn't say anything. I dipped back into the sadness. "Nothing, nothing, nothing I ever did or said was ever good enough for her. Nothing."

Marion's murmur encouraged me to go on. "She only had contempt for me and Gram. We never could measure up to her standards, to her performance. We never had anything to offer her. I mean, what can you give someone who's got it all? can do it all? knows it all?"

"Clearly she wasn't perfect."

"She sure as hell tried to be. If there were any chinks in her armor she never showed them to me—maybe to John, maybe to Dad."

"Had you planned to say something at her retirement party?"

I nodded. Recalling what, I winced.

"What?"

"I was going to read a poem."

"A poem you wrote?"

"Naw—I can't write poetry. It was a poem by Emily Dickinson."

"What about?"

"Friendship." I started sobbing again. This sadness didn't go as deep as the earlier but it felt heavy with some of the same despair. After wiping my eyes and blowing my nose, I said, "I was kind of hoping that once she retired, we could become friends."

"Equals?"

"Yeah. Able to share. Fat chance. She was gone before we even had a chance to get to know each other." And I went off on another crying jag.

I wonder if I'm premenstrual.

At the end Marion said something really nice, she said that it was such a shame that the rest of the family couldn't receive the gift John and I had prepared for them, the music and the dance, because of what they could have learned from us about friendship and equality and diversity and disregard for appearances. She said it was a tragedy we had been silenced that way. I agree.

April:

"Well, I wrote it," I say, holding up my letter to Mom. My enthusiasm almost embarrasses me. I am the good girl again, trying to please Marion. To my surprise, she doesn't ask to read it. Doesn't she care what it says?

"How do you feel?"

"Kind of empty," I admit. I realize my eagerness to share this with her is covering up a big hole. The pit again? Fear of something. "Last session was quite a purge."

She nods sympathetically. Isn't she going to tell me what's going on?

"Now what?" I can feel myself closing down. Why?

"Did it bring her closer or make her feel more distant?"

"Well, that's funny—because part of her suddenly seemed just like a figment of my imagination and another part of her became much more real."

"Which was which?"

"Well, by the time I finished writing it—and I didn't hold back, I mean why should I, she'll never see it—the remote monster part of her—the Queen—kind of toppled over, like one of those headless Greek statues. And the part of her I knew at the end—the vulnerable, open, dying part—became more real, more present. But why should that be? I knew the first for years and the other, only a very short time."

"As long as you were still angry at the first, you couldn't quite accept the other—maybe."

"Yeah—I couldn't quite accept it—it felt a little like she was pulling a fast one on me."

"What do you think happened when Bea was alone with John in the hospital room?"

That sterile room? They didn't talk—about his illness, her self-imposed exile, other people, his being gay, her arrogance, the anger between them—no, they didn't talk. They didn't even forgive each other. Seeing his pain, she put her arms around him; feeling her tenderness, he curled into her lap. Their mutual moans and sighs, their little sounds of release, relief, and comfort became a hum, a form of music. "I don't know," I say, with tears in my eyes, "I guess she finally heard his song."

"Can you imagine her sharing your dance too?"

I wince away from that suggestion. "Not yet."

"Maybe you're afraid if you become close to the one part of her, the vulnerable her, you might become too much like the other, the mean part.

That's it. The fear. Becoming like her. I notice how Marion notices how my eyes light up. It's odd to have someone my equal—or better—so tuned to my every mood. Most of my students are alert to my every move—but I don't take it personally. Of course, it's her job to tune in to her clients.

"How like her don't you want to be?"

"Oh god." I roll my eyes toward heaven. "Let me count the ways."

She smiles. "Ok, count."

The need to be superior, the need to put others down, the need to be better than other women—the compulsion to become a queen."

"And the sting that goes with that?"

"Aw yes. Do you know that queen bees only sting their rivals? But I wasn't her rival. John wasn't her rival. Dick was the one who was panting to take over from her."

"Aren't daughters always their mother's rival in some way?"

"But I wasn't competitive with her. We have completely different personalities. I'm not talented like she is, or ambitious either. If I've got to be a bee, I'm just a happy worker."

"But daughters are their mothers' replacements. There's rivalry in that."

"I wouldn't step into her shoes for a million daughters." I catch myself too late and laugh. "A million dollars, I mean."

Of course she leaps upon this Freudian slip. "Is that why you're afraid to have children?"

"Did I say I was afraid? I've got children—look at all kids I teach."

"Bea was a teacher too. You weren't afraid to share that role with her."

"No. It was like she had a whole classroom full of daughters—and not enough time for any of us."

"But you were her only daughter."

"Tell me." It feels a little like we're running in circles. What's at the center of the circle? A hole? "What's going on?"

Marion shakes her head. "Lots. But one thing I feel with you is a reluctance to claim that role adult women have traditionally held."

"But Mom was a pioneer, a tradition breaker."

"In some ways. But she wasn't exactly a new breed. She was more of a mutation. And in some ways you might have preferred a traditional mom—someone who was home more, someone who was there for you."

"Hmmm." Am I such a reactionary? "Someone who was someone else, you mean. Because even when Mom was home—when we were little—she wasn't really there, she was always up to something else."

"I guess the real question for you is not whether you can change the past, whether you can have a different mom, but who you want to be yourself."

"I sure don't want to be a traditional woman!"

"But if you claim a new power, you may have risk using your sting."

"I'm not willing to hurt someone the way she hurt me."

"It's hard to be intimate without causing some pain."

"It's different between equals."

"So maybe the question is not about pain but about equality."

"Yeah, maybe. Who knows?" Suddenly I'm weary of it all.

"What'd you do with your inheritance from her?"

This seemed an odd question at that point. "I bought myself a new car and then gave most of it away. I saved a little. It's helping pay for this therapy as a matter of fact. Why do you ask?"

"Curiosity, partially. Wondering to what extent you have rejected what you inherited from your mother."

"About eighty per cent. Some of it you just can't get rid of, you know."

She smiled. "I know. The older I get, the more people say I look like my mother. Well, you're probably not going to figure it out all by yourself."

Is she questioning my ability to climb out of this hole? "Whatdaya mean?"

"Oh just that there must be a million of us women our age trying to resolve this issue at the moment."

Oh. "You too?"

"Yeah." She grinned. "And one thing I've figured out—if we try to imitate our mothers' example, we'll quickly find ourselves obsolete. To honor our parents is not the same as repeating their mistakes. Even their successes were for a different time, a different place."

"That's a relief."

"Seems like what you did with the twenty percent of your inheritance is buy some independence and some healing, and you really didn't reject the rest, you just allowed yourself to do something with it she hadn't allowed from you."

"What's that?"

"Be generous."

I felt a spurt of tears. "Yeah, mostly she either cut us off or took what she needed without asking or thanking us."

"Maybe because that's what people had done to her."

This was the first time Marion had taken Mom's side. And it felt ok. "I think that's why I felt bad about that incident at the cabin—you know, where I couldn't hug her back. That was the first time she was receptive to me, the first time she made herself vulnerable to what I had to give her—a whole-hearted embrace, and I couldn't do it."

"Yeah, well, those things take practice."

BEE LORE

"Up to the time of her mating, [the worker bees] took little notice of [the queen bee], or were aggressive toward her, but now she produces a scent which causes them to turn and face her if she is close, thus forming a ring of workers...called her 'retinue' by the beekeeper. These are not the same workers for very long, however, for as she moves around, those she comes close to will turn to face her, but those at her rear are left behind and move away to continue other jobs. While workers are in her retinue, they lick her, clean her, and feed her, mainly on bee milk. The licking is very important because it is by doing this that they obtain various substances from the queen which control their behavior." (Ted Hooper, *Guide to Bees and Honey*)

Corey's notes: Probably the best thing about bees, of course, is honey. Not only does it taste good, but it's good for you. And if you can believe the ads about bee pollen, it's the secret of eternal youth. And wax for candles is another bee product worth noting. Honey for food, wax for candles: sweetness and light, what more could you ask for? But look what's happening—I'm focusing on what they produce. It's so work-ethic—and bees are busy enough as it is. Ironic how bees don't stand up for being, they're so busy doing (except for the drones who don't really get positive press for just being).

Turns out the queen bee isn't any different at first from a worker bee. Her egg is just treated differently, housed in a bigger cell, fed a special royal jelly. Although the best queens are raised in large hives with lots of pollen, *"good queens can be produced in less than ideal conditions as long as reasonable care is taken to prevent chilling."*

At first it seems that the queen is quite the privileged one. *"She is the most important bee in the colony, both to the hive and to the beekeeper. She is mother [or sister] of every bee in the hive: the whole inheritance of all members of the colony comes through her. This means the working quality, the temper, and the characteristics of the colony come from the queen. Change the queen and within a couple of months you have a completely new colony with, perhaps, quite a different temperament."*

And from another source: *That single female, the queen "is indispensable. She alone lays the eggs that produce successive generations of workers...She is the source of life to the hive and even more: for...the consciousness of her presence is the cohesive force that binds the colony together and keeps this complex organization running smoothly."* (Arthur Dines, *Honeybees from Close Up*)

Wow/Mom. But then there's the down side. When you look at the queen, what does she really do? The only times she gets to leave the hive is the one time she mates and then only in an emergency if she has to lead the swarm to find a new hive. The rest of the time all she does is lay the right kind of eggs in the right kind of cells, over and over and over.

And in typical systems theory fashion, *"she herself is ruled by the life of the hive."* She exercises no real control over their communal life. A queen in name only—and who gave her that name? All these books so far are by men. *"The queen is more servant to the hive than sovereign, with little, if any, control over her life and destiny, living at the convenience and tolerance of the colony."* (William Longgood, *The Queen Must Die*)

How can we figure out the difference between caring that is healthy, and caring that is unhealthy. Some of the most obsessed of us caregivers are called "saints." How much of this is biological—part of our inheritance as females, whether animal or insect—and how much of it is out of the minds of men?

Well, now, let's just read on here. Although selfless and selfish, sacrifice and narcissism, seem to be intimately entwined for a lot of us, ultimately that question is beside the point when it comes to the poor queen bee.

"Sunny days among the flowers are not for her. She normally receives a great deal of attention and her very presence has a vital effect on all the bees, but should she begin to fail in her job, the colony would soon produce a successor and discard her without ceremony." (Dines)

"There is little sentiment in a hive. The motto, indelibly and invisibly etched in bee genes, is 'work or die.'" [What is this, some kind of WASP projection?] *"Hive values are such that when a bee no longer can fly and be an asset to the colony, she will remove herself from the hive rather than be a burden. If she lacks the grace to commit suicide or to depart of her own will,* [the grace?] *she will be kicked out of the hive or killed outright by those she served so faithfully when she could. Human societies have no monopoly on ingratitude and treachery."* (Longgood)

And judging from the recent practice of laying people off just before their pensions come due, human society has not in fact progressed much beyond the insects. This does not bode well for the queen, especially the unconventional queen: *"Bees do not expect to see mother dashing about and may jump on her and sting before they realize who she is."*

"Queens can fail and become uneconomical at any age and at any time of year. The speed at which queens fail can vary considerably." (Hooper)

"A queen marked for execution is usually assassinated by the entire colony in a formalized death ritual known as balling the queen. Her only offense probably is that she is no longer able to lay enough eggs to satisfy her daughters [aha, do I detect some misogyny here? Every other time, they're workers; suddenly, they're "daugh-

ters"?], *now turned executioners. All members of the colony participate. They form a solid ball around their mother, pressing it harder and harder. The ball becomes progressively smaller as it squeezes in until the queen is crushed, suffocated or starved."*

If we've got to be insects, what about dragonflies?

Small comfort that by killing mom the bees may be wiping out their only source of nourishment: *"Killing a queen is a monstrous act for bees. Usually it happens only in moments of great stress, in panic, rage, by accident or calculation, if the colony is dissatisfied with her performance* [That pretty much covers it for all the abused, battered, and murdered wives too*]; in the later instance a successor queen raised by the colony is waiting to replace the failing or rejected sovereign. A queen marked for death or killed in pique or panic may be stung fatally by the workers, but this is rare at best. Some authorities insist it never happens. No individual or 'hit squad' apparently wants to take on such a horrendous responsibility as regicide.* [Matricide, maybe.] *By this rash act of aggression…a colony may destroy not only its queen, but its means of existence."* (Longgood)

As Alice in Wonderland says, "I tried to make it come out, 'How doth the little busy bee' but it came out all different." Quite different.

The bee's dance is fabulous—a very high form of communication. Somehow by dancing in a figure eight (a symbol of eternity, the sacred lemniscule when turned on its side), wagging its belly and whirring its wings at a certain tempo, the bee can signal the source of honey in relation to the angle of the sun, which is always changing. Let's see what this book says about it: *"The sun is moving all the while but the bee makes allowances for this movement, adjusting its dance to the lapse of time between flying home and dancing."* [The lapse of time between flying home and dancing—I wonder if there's any statute of limitations on that or if you can just fade away without ever dancing. What if there's no home to fly back to?]

The dancing bee gives samples of nectar to other bees so they'll know what kind of pollen to look for. *"The followers are therefore provided with the direction to fly, the distance to the food, the type of food to seek, its scent, and in the case of nectar, its taste and sugar concentration."* Not only is the bee sharing its dance, while making its own music, it is sharing food as well. Kind of a nifty synthesis of the aesthetic and the practical. Mom had that mix. Teaching is sort of like a bee dance—a combo of entertainment and survival training.

How about the wings? They work like oars in a boat? Ah, here's an interesting point: *"Their wings beat about 200 times a minute, which musicians say is in the key of C below middle C."* So their wings not only let them fly but make music as well. The hum of the bee is like the hum of the universe, the Om at the heart of things. Hmmm. So I guess the bee dances to the sound of her own music. Sounds like marching to the beat of a different drummer, but that cliche hardly seems to fit the life of a bee.

Guess what I just read? One bee buzzing around in a huge cathedral is equal to the amount of matter in an atom. We must be so much lighter than we feel! I wonder if that's equivalent to the proportion of sound in a note of music. The rest is silence?

And look at this: bees' eyes see a different part of the spectrum than we do—they can't see red as we can, but they can see ultra-violet while we can't. Makes them sound like a higher order—we see red all the time but we can't hardly tolerate the color of purple. Ah, listen to this, from a woman at last: *"Being one of the few preservatives the ancients knew, along with salt, honey was widely regarded as the substance of resurrection magic. In Asia Minor from 3500 to 1750 B.C. the dead were embalmed in honey and placed in fetal position in burial vases, ready for rebirth…Myths present many symbolic assurances that the Goddess would restore life to the dead through her magic 'bee balm.' The bee was rightly looked upon as a symbol of the feminine potency of nature."* (Barbara Walker, *The Women's Encyclopedia of Myths and Secrets*)

Ah, yes, but what about her sting? Bee venom, although in smaller doses, is as poisonous as snake venom. It causes painful swelling, a rash, loss of consciousness and possible death.

I guess if I were a bee, I might like a stinger. Look at how easily people step on spiders, most of whom have no weapon and many of whom are actually servants of the greater good.

But get this. The queen herself *"will die rather than sting to defend herself."* *Noblesse obliges?* Clearly, I myself am not cut out to be a queen. The last time some guy grabbed me, I kicked for the groin—missed, of course. I'm still not sure I could go for the eyes.

Oh no, the queen never uses her sting except against a rival. A worthy opponent.

Why, then, did she sting me?

COREY'S CHOICE

Corey shoved her heaviest bag into the compartment above and stuffed the lighter one under the seat in front. Good that she'd packed so efficiently, and that clothes for a tropical climate were so light. Too bad there hadn't been time to check the bags. Traffic into the airport had been much worse than they anticipated. Thank god for Steve. Wary as she was of depending upon him, he was proving remarkably trustworthy.

She sank into the window seat, relieved to collapse after the frantic drive, but unable to relax. She still clutched the newspaper Steve had given her just before she hugged him. She couldn't concentrate now, so she tucked it in the seat pocket for later, when the hours would drag on and she would feel trapped in this cramped space. Now she could hardly sit still, she was so excited to be going on this trip, so anxious about what she'd discover when she got there, so worried about how she'd adjust to the people, the heat, the bugs, the food.

She glanced at the man next to her, wondering where he was going. A businessman apparently, setting up his computer soon after he'd sat down and strapped on his seat belt. She might have preferred a more grandmotherly type for a seatmate, for this trip anyway. She supposed Gram was with her, in spirit at least.

As the plane taxied out to the runway, all she could think of was what she'd left behind: Steve's reassuring grin and thumbs up as she waved at him before heading down the umbilical tunnel into the plane. Would he be there for her when she returned? Sally's anxious expression just before she hugged Corey goodbye and whispered, "Have fun, but don't forget to come back." Corey wondered, if there were orphans to be adopted, whether she could persuade Sally to take one or two. Then her mind wandered back toward her job: Should she ask for a raise when she returned in September or should she file a grievance about her overcrowded classroom? Should she become more active in the teachers' union? How she could persuade the school system to provide more equipment and time for hands-on learning?

As the plane took off, these routine concerns dropped away and she faced the larger issue propelling her on this journey. The pregnancy scare with its surprising disappointment had forced her to face her potential as a mother. *Mother* was not an abstraction. Mother was Bea with all her tyrannies, frailties, and quirks. Odd re-reading that journal she'd kept back then, after Bea's death when she was seeing Marion—how detached she felt from the person who'd written it. Now she saw Bea in a different light.

Without a dramatic, conscious moment, she must have forgiven her. The older she got, the more she could understand Bea's complexity, her contradictions. But re-reading her bee lore had convinced Corey that whatever the organic pattern, she didn't want to be an active reproducer. She didn't want to give birth.

It wasn't hard to come up with reasons, although which ones really counted still baffled her. She knew too much about the environment, overpopulation and sustainability to believe that bringing more children into the world would be a contribution. She knew too much about genetics to think that her particular bloodstream was uniquely valuable; in any case, it was already being extended by nieces and nephews. And much as she loved individual members, she had no great impulse to perpetuate her family dynamics, or even to play a variation on that theme.

I've already chosen to relate differently to the next generation, she realized. *Teaching's demanding too, but it's more objective, less selective. I've got to reach out to* all *the kids in my class, especially the ones with lousy parents. I don't own them, their blood doesn't flow through my veins, they're not going to take care of me in my old age. But I can make a difference in their lives, more lives than I can physically produce.* Of course she could be both a teacher and a mother, but that hadn't happened naturally or spontaneously. Without some serious restructuring of her life in ways over which she had little control, it was less and less likely to occur.

Instead by taking this trip she was reaching out to even more kids, children who might need her help more than the lonely and needy kids at school. She was also reaching out to another culture. Maybe there she'd find the child of her dreams; maybe that child would find her. Then she might consider adopting. But was it right to drag a child out of his native land? Would transplanting him into alien soil so rich the child could never return home do more harm than good? Adoption was as mixed a bag as giving birth. She better stick to teaching and exploring.

Ever since Gram died, Corey had felt a primal pull to create or patchwork together some kind of family of her own. Right now it seemed that would take a miracle. She had no idea what kind of father Steve would be. He liked kids. But so had her father and he'd been as remote as a good father could be—and that wasn't entirely Bea's fault. Even though Steve was only a couple of years younger than she, he seemed still a boy, somehow.

Corey was fascinated by how the plane's shadow shrank to a pinpoint as they rose in the air. It took her a while longer to notice the sphere of light which seemed to be following them. Surrounding its glow was a full circle rainbow, like the halo around the moon on a humid night. At first she thought it was sunlight seen from a high altitude—from the sun's own point of view perhaps. Then she observed that the light itself seemed to be traveling. It remained consistent even as it adapted its shape to the contours of the fields or buildings it crossed.

She particularly liked how it shone on water, shimmering down the line of a river before traveling on at the same rate of speed as the plane itself. At that she realized it *was* the plane itself—or its reflection, what Marion might call its "bright shadow." Oddly enough, the light reflected had more endurance than the somber image, which disappeared at a certain altitude. Sunlight bouncing off the plane's metal surface was more powerful than the plane's own shadow.

As they angled out across the ocean, this guardian angel trailed along over the waves, holding its circle complete while adjusting the ins and outs of its sphere to the texture of the water. When they rose above the clouds, its aura was so enhanced by the misty globular context of cloud that it seemed to be dancing, to and fro, up and down, even as the plane itself soared straight as an arrow. Corey wondered briefly if this lively light was her grandmother's spirit, still partially present. She'd gone so quickly, too quickly.

The plane was headed for London's Heathrow Airport. From there Corey would board another plan bound for India, where she'd spend the summer as an exchange teacher in a school for outcast and orphaned children. Even with friends to send her off and friends to greet her, she felt as if she were flying solo, propelled by a dream. There's nothing quite so unique, so indescribable, she thought, as motivation born from a dream.

She'd dreamt John had been reborn in India. Not that he was a little Buddha or anything like that. In the dream she was in some tropical environment, which she recognized upon awakening as India. There she met a young boy about four or five. He looked very poor and rather malnourished but there was a light in his eyes, which spoke memories to her, and when she woke up she knew he was John. She felt enormous relief that he was still alive, somehow, such relief that she wept. Even though she still practiced Buddhist meditation, she didn't believe in reincarnation. She wasn't sure she even believed in life after death except in the most nebulous of ways.

Imagining India, she'd thought of her friend Sita, an exchange teacher from India whose mother, a follower of Ghandi, ran a school for outcast children in South India. Last year Sita returned to help her aging mother with the school. Before she left, she invited Corey to visit her there. Corey was intrigued but didn't seriously consider it until the dream. It was too far away, too expensive, the poverty too depressing.

After the dream, she researched teacher exchange programs. She applied and was awarded a grant to go. With more energy than she usually had, she took care of getting a passport, shots, information about the country, plane tickets, tropical clothing, language books.

Imagining what lay before her was harder than remembering what she left behind. Restless, she shifted her focus to the newspaper stuffed in the seat pocket. One article about a revolutionary process called "blood conversion" caught her attention. She read every detail about how various blood types could be changed into the common type O negative. She learned about the invention of a machine which used an enzyme to strip away the extra sugar molecules which created other types like her own B. Creating this common ground of blood, the scientists claimed, would permit easy transfusion, prevent contamination of blood sources, facilitate the sharing of blood.

All to the good, she thought, until the phrase "wash the unwanted molecule away" jumped out. Was this another kind of genetic engineering, an attempt to make us all conform to a single uniform standard, or did it symbolize a potential for democratic communion? Did O negative stand for zero progress or for unity? John was like an unwanted molecule who was washed away. A brown child whom she'd bring into her mostly white community might feel the same way: outcast again.

Corey tried to imagine the Indian myth of Indira's web, popular with some western quantum physicists: the universe as a net full of faceted gems, each one unique, and each one reflecting the multicolored lights of the others. The earth seen from space looked like a jewel. Corey searched through the dark screen of window for the single gem which had followed them as the flight began. Disappeared. Of course, now, in the dark, it would be gone. Beyond the dark clouds was a diffusion of silver grey light which hinted of a moon. No stars she could see.

Her mind wandered out through the weave of air, water and cloud which filled the dark around the plane. Maybe Type O Negative blood is like the dark, like soil, like a womb, the chaotic ocean out of which unique lights of different shapes, patterns and colors are born. If so, I'm swimming through it now.

About the Author

Margaret Blanchard lives in a small Vermont town. She is professor of graduate studies at Vermont College of Union Institute & University and the author of three other published novels, as well as three books on intuition and one book of poetry. She also works with stained glass and photography.

978-0-595-36338-4
0-595-36338-5